HOTHOUSE BLOOM

HOTHOUSE BLOOM

AUSTYN WOHLERS

HUB CITY PRESS
SPARTANBURG, SC

Copyright © 2025
Austyn Wohlers

All rights reserved. No part of this book may be reproduced in any form or by any electronic means, including information storage and retrieval systems, without permission in writing from the publisher, except by a reviewer, who may quote brief passages in a review.

Design Lead: Meg Reid
Hub City Editor: Katherine Webb-Hehn
Copy Editor: Iza Wojciechowska
Managing Editor: Kate McMullen
Marketing Assistant: Julie Jarema
Cover Painting: Daniel Ablitt

Library of Congress Cataloging-in-Publication Data

Names: Wohlers, Austyn, 1996- author
Title: Hothouse bloom / Austyn Wohlers.
Description: Spartanburg, SC : Hub City Press, 2025.
Identifiers: LCCN 2025024438 (print)
LCCN 2025024439 (ebook)
ISBN 9798885740500 (hardback)
ISBN 9798885740616 (ebook)
Subjects: LCGFT: Novels
Classification: LCC PS3623.O346 H68 2025 (print)
LCC PS3623.O346 (ebook)
DDC 813/.6—dc23/eng/20250602

LC record available at https://lccn.loc.gov/2025024438
LC ebook record available at https://lccn.loc.gov/2025024439

Epigraph from *This World We Must Leave and Other Essays* by Jacques Camatte. Anti-copyright 1995, Jacques Camatte & Autonomedia.

FIRST EDITION
Printed and bound in the USA

HUB CITY PRESS
153 N. Spring Street
Spartanburg, SC 29306
864.577.9349 | www.hubcity.org

To José Quiroga

"Here it is not a question of death as the extinction of life, but of death-in-life, death with all the substance and power of life. The human being is dead and no more than a ritual of capital."

—Jacques Camatte

1

She was born for (and was always seeking) a world of immense gentleness. She was always trying to prolong the hours into all sixty of their gradient minutes, and to stretch the minutes into the full halo of their sixty seconds. To expand her understanding of a single instant out into infinitude. She wanted to coat each one with the secret heart of things, with a kind of vitality that came from somewhere beyond her, so she could someday say that she had lived a rich life full of affect. Yet she was always envying those to whom things simply happened.

Conversely, her life was unflowing: nothing "simply happened" to her. Something about the world had never seemed right by her, she wasn't sure what. Her life was aimless by every visible yardstick: others had their lives, loves, adventures and tragedies…once she'd had the inclination to paint, whatever that might have entailed. She lacked vision. Besides, that wasn't what she wanted, not exactly. But while deaths in her family tended to pass consequenceless—none of them knew each other, they never held funerals, like hawks they flew and fell alone—it happened that a relative had left her the orchard like a hand serenely extended. It appeared to her as cloudfingers stretching down from the blue, waiting. A gigantic white sketch of a hand. The way out.

She fled the city in her dark green car glittering with water droplets kicked up by her tires. The roads were rough and unfamiliar. The fog was thick. Whenever it cleared she watched the buildings morph in and out of their rural forms. Then everything closed up again, the world opaque and thistle gray, and she drove incomprehensibly forward, then again the wide yellow flood of her headlights penetrated a weak sphere of fog and illuminated the soil in the earth and in the hills, a cold and snowless streaming world, she saw green, some gray, early specks of pink and orange wildflowers in the rocks. It was March. Sometimes the clouds above her would double over and drive clear spears of water into the earth, further limiting her vision as she drove on and on, slowly so she didn't crash into something, into the unknown.

Her back ached. Her neck, her shoulders. She hadn't stopped yet. Because she was afraid of getting lost in the country—no signal, the darkness falling, the unfamiliar landscape, forced to sleep in her car or in some strange field. She had left early. The light kept rising.

Ambiently she began to wonder what Joe, the relative, had been like. As a kid she used to forget if he was her grandfather, great-uncle, or distant cousin…her mother would have to remind her he was her grandfather.

He was the same as all of them. Her family was like the facets of a diamond, glimmery. All faced outward. And what was the unknown center? And their lives projected outward and away from one another, like a bright light reflected off all its surfaces at once. Some hurdled off into the heavens—others dead into the earth.

They were cold like diamonds too. There had been no great fallout, but some unsourceable hostility kept them all at odds with one another, as though none of them were meant for human company. Her mother was cold, her uncles and her aunts were cold. The rest of them. Anna herself was cold, she knew it, and so was Joe, so she had heard, though she could recall sweet and ambiguously formed memories of snowball fights, warm fires, afternoons drawing with her colored pencils on the wood floor, and a few handwritten letters he had sent her about the weather, which plants were blooming, the deer at the edge of the woods, the family of raccoons beneath the floorboards…she'd almost never responded. After all, she was just a little girl. She couldn't remember his face. She didn't know why it was all hers.

With an enormous blank force, she obliterated the thoughts. The why of it didn't matter. All that mattered was the image of the orchard, itself unformed, coalescing, metamorphosing.

And now the day was dawning and its psychedelic colors were dyeing the fog: lilac, rose, tigerlily, marigold…she heard crows, other birds. Encouraged by the light, she sped up. She thought her vision was clearing. She felt a wash of hope bubble up inside her, excitement, light emerging and coloring her body like a prism. Where before it had felt dense and dark as iron.

She felt her tire slip, righted it. Her car seemed to drift as if on ice. It was water. She drove with traction and then slid again, tried to break, glided luxuriously, like a figure skater, and then lost in the fog her car bucked, she wasn't sure if it had gone up or down, she couldn't see. She leaned into the brake, begging it to stop, there was a blow against the metal. The car skidded to a halt somewhere between the grass and the shoulder lane.

Her hands shook lightly on the wheel. Cars flew by, metal sounds and colors.

She stayed still for three minutes before getting out of the car.

All around her was fog, fog, fog.

She crouched down to inspect the grille. It was caked in some brownish substance, though she wasn't sure if it was blood or mud. She touched it. She felt its thickness. It was mud. Of course it would be mud. But could mud mask blood? And isn't that a new dent? She looked pitifully off into the woods but saw no wounded animal. She looked behind her car for potholes, but the fog confronted her like a phantom and she grew afraid.

She tried to skim the mud off with the ice scraper. No luck. She returned to the car. The gas light was on.

Her hands trembling with guilt and fatigue, she put her hazards on and crawled up the shoulder to the first exit. She pulled into a gas station with a faded red sign. Inside, the white floors were vinyl-tiled and the low egg-colored shelves were stocked with junk food, car tools, canned meat, plastic-wrapped pastries. The fluorescent light hummed like a beehive. Everything was bright and hurt her eyes. A woman sat at the cash register, looking down, and behind her in a pen a brown dog, sensing something, raised its head to gaze at Anna. Its tags jingled. It thumped its tail.

Then the woman asked, looking up from her phone: "Need something?"

"Could I get twenty dollars of gas on pump two?"

She took the bill from Anna's hand and put it in the register. The woman had condensed features, hard and rosy like a small pink rock. She was playing a game on her phone.

"I think I may have hit something," Anna confessed. "An animal."

The woman glanced up, looked superficially sorrowful, sighed.

"It happens. Animal control comes by for roadkill twice a week."

So it was confirmed. Anna went back to her car. So it happens. She put the nozzle in the tank. First contact. But she told herself she was unfazed, glanced at the field beside the gas station, a small and slowly greening patch of grass enclosed by a chain link fence. Suppressing a heat inside her she looked at the field as the gas flowed. Vaguely she felt a longing for penance, as though by killing something on her way to construct the new life she had committed some act of great evil. The pump stopped. She got inside the car and turned her key in the ignition. My first act in the incandescent country. A murder. And then that awful artifice. She backed out and returned uncertainly to the road. Her hands were shaking again on the wheel. She felt embarrassed of her humanity, as though it were a violent and intrusive thing. Get a grip! And she did. Now she held the wheel with new strength. As she returned to the highway her expression grew serious, tangible. Perhaps the whole incident was the old life symbolically fading away…After all, I'm at the threshold, aren't I? That's what I can make of that. Things are about to be so different. The slate wiped clean. I'm not yet at the orchard. The unblemished life, life free from human error. It's starting: now.

Meanwhile there was the real problem of arriving at the orchard. The threat of getting lost, the sensation it might not even be real. It attached itself to no reality in her mind. Instead she was thinking: within me there is a furtive world of streams and life-burgeonings, I will no longer be paralyzed, things will flow freely into me, I will live the existence I have yearned for. In weeks the butterflies will be migrating in the bushes, and I will be alone in the countryside. Look, and I feel myself smiling: the fog lifts.

She took her exit.

Here the heights of the hills were dizzying, the curvatures of the earth so enormous it seemed the ground itself was warping as in a dream, or as though she were racing like a little green marble down to the bottom of a massive glass ball. Her stomach lurched. Whirring by her through the car window were the bare branches of juniper trees, checkerberry bushes, rosebay and bracken ferns, everything melting into smudged strokes of life from within her speed. A grocery store, a university, businesses, bricks, town houses: the little buildings of the town watching her from their distance. She glanced out at them. Long stretches of muddy earth, gravel. Big fields full of machines and vegetables. Standing animals. Unfinished roads.

As she slowed her car down a gravel path, she rolled her windows down. The car sputtered in the mud. It seemed weak. She descended into the field of farms the way a diver arrives in a clear blue pool.

Hers was on a little hill. In the sunlight she could see gleaming threads of young spiderwebs connecting bushes to structures like fishing lines. Gnats flew in circles like dust motes. She heard the black calls of crows. She looked for them. There they were, a flock on a roof. Some scattered. The farmstead confronted her like an abandoned world. Like an animal she had been deposited into a habitat of whose history she was unaware, yet could sense. Rotting wood, untrimmed branches. Flaking paint. Trees eaten a little by—something.

But for now she was looking at the hot-looking light falling thickly on the ground like wax. Sunshine was wrapping itself around the trees and the buildings, assuming the shape of objects. Here she could grow roots, she who had always been rootless. Abjure her fellow man, she who had been abjured. Prolong time by entering a world of timelessness, or at least one where time passed on a different scale. As if she herself were surrounded in those thick sheets of light, the shadow of the failed life dissipated. Here she could hide her nothingness from the world, her shame. It was simply something that had happened, and was now over.

She parked in the raw dirt and turned off the engine.

2

And opened the car door.

She was encircled by the farmstead. Above her she saw a sparkling metal pinwheel spinning blithely on the roof of the cabin, which was made from wood and stone, with birch planks painted in patches of primary colors, wisps of green plants clinging to the cracks in the walls...there was an herb garden flowing out from the kitchen window, dead rosemary, dead mint, unknown bushes...a grove of bamboo extending out from the side of the house like an angel's emerald wing. A clothesline clamped by glittering brass pins drawn taut between two branches, chopped firewood, red and blue rain barrels, white wood sheds, a barn with a bird coop, a gray greenhouse with a green roof and a yellow door... a tarnished spigot whose water seemed to run somewhere into the thick pines that formed the woods around the property, though now, directly above her, the sky was blue and clear, the tin roofs gleamed palely, distantly she could sense the river, distantly she could see on the horizon the mountains and valleys sketched by the sun like tinted glass.

She waded through the farm as if in water, thinking. She ran her fingers over the wood and metal of its incomprehensible tools.

Long before anything "went wrong" the idea of flight had been within her. She had always felt the rituals of life did not make sense. She was afraid of making wrong decisions and therefore afraid of life itself. Everything that happened felt abstractedly wrong: whenever the world commanded her to do something she would think "why should I" not out of rebellion but despair.

At times she had caught glimpses of those sparkling instances she would have liked to shore up over herself, but the feeling would never last. It seemed to her that the solution lay somewhere at the boundaries of her consciousness, only sometimes perceptible, as though her mind were a room with translucent walls where deliverance lay in the forms and colors obscured by its semitransparency. Her life had been defined by halfhearted attempts at grasping those forms. Experiments in love, generosity, art, work, friendship: they'd all only exacerbated things. Painting had come close—she had hoped it might help to pour her consciousness onto surfaces—but art always erupted outward. Friendship had come close as well, especially with those who shared her unease, but some fundamental misunderstanding would eventually return everyone to the oppressive fabric of the world.

Therefore it had been easy for her to sever ties with spectacular indifference. She told few of the people with whom she had populated her life that she was retreating. Those she did tell she seemed happy to forget just moments after speaking obliquely about her inheritance. In fact she liked the sweet pain of abandoning those closest to her, especially the man against whom she had always felt defined, her selfhood enclosed by his in the imperceptible and boring ways romance conquers and extinguishes a life.

It was all a way of preventing the mark of defeat from staining her, of stepping freshbirthed into a new world as if from a void. And with a disembodied love she was stepping into that new world—a world of love for space instead of being—a world away from everything and everybody—a bright, empty world where the "something-off" was absent.

Because here the sun is shining silently, she thought. And she looked at the sun.

Because here the sun is shining silently, far from that unbearable and indeterminate thing. Because here I am barely a person, and nobody knows a thing about who I was. In a place belonging to me and me alone, so overabundant with life that it's functionally nothing, happily indifferent to me except where it demands to be touched.

Yet the air seemed heavy with an absence. Walking around it was hard to see the spatula in the sink, the dents in the pillows, the imperfectly made bed and not feel as though she were in someone else's home. There was a sense of trespass and of presence, as though the true owner of the orchard might appear around any corner.

She entered the barn. It was dark inside. She smelled a warm, musky smell, so sour it was almost sweet. She found the light and pulled the chain. There were rabbits still as sculptures in rectangular cages, a vertical field of spiderwebs, dusty barrels of feed in the corner, ducks moving in the coop. They quacked at her through the chicken wire, and when she opened the coop door, half the birds blackish green like moss on a wet rock, pretty, the others brown with blank black eyes like buttons sewn on the faces of old stuffed animals—they gently gathered near her left hand.

Anna bent down to stroke the nearest hen's feathers. Its eyes closed obediently, squinting. Gentle, not like a bird. Like a dog. She looked at her bare hand. Her mother had described Joe's particular iciness as the iciness of the inconsistent: he was the type to reach out when ignored but withdraw when shown affection. Impossible to love wholly. But in interfacing with the ducks it seemed to Anna as though the ghost or memory of a love was lingering. Food fed from the left palm. Instinctively the animals trusted her.

She let the ducks into the run, scooped pellets out of a barrel. She approached the feeder.

Abruptly she saw that the ducks had both food and water.

She checked the rabbits and it was the same.

She quickly left the barn and shut the door.

She looked around.

The crows went on cawing.

And across the grass one of the feral cats was watching her, its body tense, mirroring hers.

The sense of trespass rose again like a red wave of shame. Who? She wondered if it was a mistake, the orchard wasn't hers, even though her keys opened the door, that's right, but…

She tried to relax her body.

The cat stayed strained. It ran off.

No, of course someone would have cared for the farm in the interim. She may have even been told. Still she looked around untrusting. She did not like the thought of someone else in her newly private world.

She walked through the tall grasses, trying to forget about it…she ran her hand along plant matter…she tried to relax into the feeling of moving through a river of heaven, as though the air and grasses here were made of the same spongy celestial substance passing invisibly through and around her body. It was quiet…she passed the garden. She listened to wind and birds. She passed the bamboo grove and saw the light had changed. Now it was a wall of serpentine. She crested the grass hill.

Here she was faced with the vast soft hills of apple trees.

She saw the artificial-looking mounds of dirt between each row, the orbed raindrops clinging to the wet skeletal branches. Some of the trees seemed to glow a ghostly blue. Strange color. She approached the orchard.

There were a few hundred of them. Berry bushes and flowers in the underbrush. And the trees lined up so precisely: no random sprawling as she saw in the herb garden. Here there was a more human geometry. The trees were planted in patterns of three and, just as she'd been told, they went: apple apple honey-locust apple apple honey locust apple apple honey locust and the honey locusts so much taller than the apple trees, yellowish chartreuse and peridot. Staring down a row of trees her heart tightened, seeing them refracted up and down with the curvature of the hill like a warped hall of mirrors. The gray-green of the branches wherever they were not ghost-blue.

She rubbed her temples. Then she squatted down and pushed her hands into the loam, feeling the wet earth and the tiny movements of things, the roughness of the straw mulch, the segments of the worms she just knew were moving beneath her body. And she herself brimming, brimming. And this even if the moments that passed became fuzzier with distance, even if they were being lost just as they were forming, and she herself extending into the air, the soil, the water, growing broader and wider, her humanity dissolving with her presence in the orchard.

On the farmstead's eight acres there would soon enough be thousands of individual fruits and all of them would look just alike. She tried to hold every apple in her mind and think of where their seeds had been and where they would be going, where they would coagulate. Apple pies, apple ciders, apple sauces, apple jellies, apple butters, candied apples, savory curry apples, apple crumbles, apple cider vinegars, raw apples eaten in huge crisp bites by children with potbellies and yellow teeth. Apples in the grocery store. Apples in the plastic grocery bag.

She tried to feel them as if growing inside her. Yes, growing painfully, as if inside her own body. Every tree looked the same to her, as though copied and pasted from the preceding trees, it was like a computer, and where was she again? Before the slow primacy of plant life that sustained and reigned over the world.

She took out her phone, where she had stored the information from the estate lawyer. Looking at his notes she tried to ascertain which apples grew where by their configuration, height, and texture. There were three principal heritage cultivars:

Ruby Beauties:
Small, conic apples which despite the name are not especially vibrant—a nice light pink, tart to eat raw but excellent in ciders. Trees have a long taproot, allowing them to easily withstand harsh weather. Resistant to scab and cedar rust. Popular with local breweries.

Federations:
Reddish-yellow, mottled. Large, hard, crunchy. Nice balance of sweetness and acidity. Cream-colored flesh. Keeps well and great for eating fresh. Trees are semi-dwarf, delicate, with vibrant pink blooms. Very susceptible to fireblight. Surround with hardier plants.

Teratourgimas:
Standard-sized, unassuming trees. The fruits are sweet, soft, striped, and extremely large, averaging nearly thirteen inches in circumference. Lauded in the region; regularly sells for $10/lb.

This last apple was hardly imaginable to her, but later in the day she found one of the Teratourgimas at the bottom of a shed's deep freezer. It was unbagged and uncovered. Just an apple, loose in the bottom of the faintly grimy freezer. Just an apple tormented by frost. It must have fallen in accidentally. She picked it up and held it burning cold in her palm, which the apple nearly completely obscured. Its redness concealed, the gigantic scarlet of the apple iced by tiny flakes of frost and slightly dented from having been dropped. This apple which was bigger than a human heart and which she had never seen in grocery stores. She looked beyond it down into the freezer, empty.

She returned her gaze to the crystal fruit. It seemed to gesture at once forward to the harvest and backward to Joe's hands, which had surely touched it, right? Someone like her had touched this apple. And there was no telling how old it really was, it may have been only a few months old or something more ancient, forgotten at the bottom of a freezer for years on end, continually crushed and obscured by whatever was on top of it, while outside generations of animals lived and died, bamboo rocketed like skyscrapers, vines extended their tendrils in multiyear conquests. Again the organization of the world was a slow confusion to her, because whatever series of events had abandoned the apple in the bottom of the freezer was inscrutable: the circumstances of life were obscured from her. So many secret histories and she was left with merely the fact of its existence.

After taking it inside the cabin and thawing it in a bowl of hot water, she took a bite. It was disgusting. The flesh was soft, brown, and bitter. The disgusting taste lingered in her mouth.

She felt guilty for having ruined something so perfect and slow. So untouched. Thinking of the animal she had killed, she thought sadly how all her actions were destructions: yes: how exerting her will upon the world was akin to destroying it.

She tried to explore some more but before she knew it the day was already ending, the sun leaching new colors as it set, and she retreated from the falling darkness to the safety of the cabin. Outside, the gigantic orchard shapeshifted like a monster in her imagination. The dark was crushing the light like a living being, the slow way a snake swallows something whole. There were too many buildings to comprehend and remember all at once, and as visible space foreclosed itself around her and made the world unknown, she understood that none of the living things around her (trees, ducks, cats, rabbits, spiders) shared her language. In fact they lived in a world that was foreign to her. One where the shadow of a hawk or the partially understood sensation of a scythe ignited fear. What ignited fear for Anna? The world growing jet black as though rotting.

The sounds that came with night. A splash of thunder. She looked outside the window. A rainy spring!

The house creaked like a ship. She locked the door. She sat down on the big gray couch, tired and afraid. She looked around at the coffee table, the other chairs, the cabinets, the dirt on the wood. All the furniture was painted with shadow. And shadows appeared as figures.

Now it was raining hard and incomprehensible sounds kept arriving from beyond the door. She found a can of soup in the cupboards. She lit the stove with a match. She shivered. She drew all the milk-white curtains.

As usual she tried to console herself. Here I can pass my life without incident, she reminded herself, surrounded and enclosed by the pines, liberated from the pressure of existing out in the open. Life will swallow me instant and slow. I just have to get used to it.

But the outside sounds muffled by rain and thunder did not go away. A shadow passed beyond the window. She surrendered to her own unease. There was definitely something moving out there in the night.

She climbed into bed and wrapped herself in the heavy darkness. Velvety, velvety. It was a stiff bed. Sometimes she would see beyond the fear and it would exhilarate her, it was a new way of being alive, a world in which something might happen to her, the door might fly open at any moment, she could even die, she could even die and nobody would know…finally exhaustion weighed down upon her. She fell asleep.

3

Not long after sunrise in the deep wet morning there was a pounding at the door. It jolted her awake. Sleepy, she thought for a moment it might be the very heartbeat of the house's wood, finally alive like everything else…She rolled over. She was still sore from driving. The room was dim and vaguely green from the sun radiating through the bamboo in the window.

She shivered out of the musty yellow sheets. Her breath seemed to coagulate in the air in front of her. She strained her body against the cold. She stumbled out into the brightness of the living room, which was in fact the brightness of the day, but her mind stayed in the night. She had had her usual dreams. Nightmares of encroachment. As a child she'd dreamed of cars crashing through the windows of her house, as an adult that some malevolent stranger would burst through the doors of her apartment. Now she dreamed of dark figures at the edges of a field.

More pounding. Her clothes were still in a bag by the front door. She put on a hat, a jacket, a second pair of pants. Someone at the door. Then she looked around for something she could use to defend herself, if it came to that. A hammer in a cabinet…She tried to peek through the window but the angle was too sharp to see who was knocking. She was unused to the nakedness of solitude, she was afraid, and the round eyes of the orchard were on her.

Ridiculous, she thought, fingering the wood handle of the hammer.

As she opened the door she was confronted with a man on the porch, compact and muscular, ruddy, his wiry curly hair drawn back into a cloudcolored ponytail, though she sensed it had been dark in his youth. He said good morning with enthusiasm and in one fluid movement tried to enter the cabin.

She shut the door halfway.

He took a step backward.

"It's Gil," he said, like she should know.

She stood watching him and held the hammer behind the door. She eyed the plastic grocery bag in his hand.

"Remind me your name? Anna?" he said. "I took care of the place after Joe died. No one told you?" He moved farther back, half out of the cabin's shadows and into light. "Just to thin buds, spray copper, make sure the pipes don't freeze."

"No, no one told me," she lied.

"Here." He dug around in his pocket. "My spare."

He gave her a key. Staring at it in the palm of her hand, she tried to set the hammer down undetected.

"I see," she said. "Come in."

He came in behind her. But after crossing the threshold of the doorway he made a small sound of surprise, turned around, and went out again mumbling about the cold. She watched him wallow through the garden. He picked up firewood from beneath the lean-to, bundling some under his arm. All around him the world was drenched, luminous, as though the rain had lathered up the stars and seeped them into everything. She saw the light atop the dew and remembered its promise to efface individuality. She was washed with calm. That's right.

She stood up straighter, as though the roots of the apple trees were shooting up through the floorboards, joining with her blood vessels.

Gil returned and moved past her to the kitchen. He set the firewood in the wood stove. "I chopped this all for you, you know!" he said in a singsong voice. He set his bag on the kitchen table, took some twigs and scraps of paper from the tinderbox, and started up a fire.

As they sat at the kitchen table, she watched him grope around for the right words.

"Well, first, Anna, my condolences," he said finally.

His eyes crinkled in pain. He reached out his palm.

"It's all right. I didn't know him."

"You didn't?"

"Not really."

"You didn't know him," he said sadly.

He looked down at his hand, a gnarled, wrinkled thing that was resting on the table in front of him. He reached over to the stove and opened a damper. The embers were glowing against the dull green paint of the kitchen and deep inside the wood stove the growing flames, like firepriests, were exorcising the purple shadows.

"I mean I hardly knew him," she offered.

Gil kept frowning. Strange to see a man mourn for and comprehend someone who was for her little more than a lucky absence. She avoided his eyes, looking down at the table.

"What about the property?"

"Not too much."

Gil shifted in his seat. "The most important thing to know is that it's a permaculture orchard, in a sense," he said. "The plot used to be much larger, in the '70s, but the university bought up most of the land for the preserve. Joe bought what was left, kept the name, changed the rest. Permaculture is…you could think of it like its own private ecosystem, everything feeding back into itself. The bamboo, the animals, the garden. Of course, the apple trees themselves Joe had trouble fully integrating into the system. They're finicky plants with a lot of pests. The trees still need irrigation, pruning, spraying, hands for the harvests. The honey locusts fix nitrogen, and there's something about the berries between the rows…"

He stared up at the ceiling with his mouth half open, counting on two fingers, thinking.

"Really, I know more about the rest of it. I helped your grandfather out in the garden all the time. My wife and I live just over there, just west of you, we raise sheep. He was a good, friendly neighbor. It's important to be friendly. You don't look too friendly yourself, not with that scowl!"

His look of sadness had evaporated. He smiled at her, his teeth a bit crooked.

"I'm kidding. You want to know what he thought of you, don't you? I think it pained him how incompletely he knew you, like he was grasping at the facts of your life from afar. How long's it been, twenty years? Twenty-five? He'd always tell Tamara and me the same story from when you were a little girl, so when you opened the door that's almost who I expected to answer: a little girl. You came here on vacation when you were seven or eight, your dad had spent all afternoon chopping wood with Joe, he was exhausted, it was snowy and bleak and dark already, but you insisted on playing some kind of board game before everyone went to sleep…you lost and cried for hours. Your mother scolded you and said you would have to learn to lose. She wanted you to be graceful. But Joe thought a young lady ought to learn to want something fiercely enough to cry if she couldn't get it. He was concerned your mother was raising a pushover. They argued about it all night after you went to bed. The next day they all found out you had an ear infection and that was probably why you had cried so much. You sucked all morning on a giant glassy icicle. Joe and his folk remedies! Anyway, from what I understand, you two eventually lost contact, as your mother withdrew, though Joe followed your art career as closely as he could with what information he could find or squeeze out of your mother. Though I suppose he stopped talking about all that a few years ago. Is that right?"

"It isn't."

They were frozen looking at each other across the table. The house creaked in the wind. They sat for a moment in silence while Anna suffered before this portrait of herself.

"I don't want to hear about any of that."

The man across from her kept moving his lips around as though he were chewing on something. His words. He smiled with some bitterness.

"Fair enough. I'll have to work with an incomplete picture," he said. "Before I forget, I brought you something."

He picked up the plastic bag and opened it up for her: lettuce, kale, batteries for a flashlight, radishes with dirt on their bright red skin. Then he shared other details of the life he seemed to think she should live, starting with how to work the wood stove and how he liked to cook the radishes; she told him some details of the inheritance, such as how the dilapidation of some of the buildings had subtracted from the value of the property. Gil made a defeated gesture and said Joe had meant to reinforce the foundation on the packing shed and the greenhouse and the barn, but had never gotten around to it; anyway, it couldn't be more than a few days' work. She had received some money along with the property, but she would need to turn a profit on the harvest. Joe had always made a profit, Gil reassured her. Their conversation grew warmer. They turned back to permaculture. Ducks instead of chickens, Gil said: better for pest control, float in a flood. Campbells for eggs, East Indies for the iridescent feathers. Beauty matters, he said winking, and he seemed to want to say more but stopped himself. You regulate the soil with other plants instead of chemical fertilizers: in the garden, the alfalfa and white clover stabilized the clay. Perennials, everywhere, perennials.

As she listened her heart stayed clenched in her throat. Here's another person, she thought. While the day is escaping me.

But she felt a bit guilty for that flash of callousness. She let him go on.

He took her outside. They toured the garden. Here's the alfalfa, mutter, ginseng, clover, woad for dye, maybe for wool from some of our sheep? Another wink. In the sunlight he was jolly. Sweet-smelling lilies, sorrel, scallions, stinging nettle, mugwort, garlic, rhubarb, tall sunchokes whose strong roots walled the weeds. These regulate soil nutrients, those attract good pollinators, and even the structure of the garden serves a purpose: rainwater swirls down its random-looking pathways so that each plant receives its share, and rain that would otherwise drown the plants drains into a puddle where it is soaked up by a verdant patch of watercress.

"Think of the movement of the water like an Incan terrace," he said at the watercress, playful, smiling again.

She did so, imagining herself far above the garden as though peering down from Andean clouds, beholding the garden as one beholds a forest…all the information was beginning to overwhelm her. She felt impatient. Here and there some plants seemed crushed, and the wet earth that held them was slightly impressed. Others were still dead from winter. When would the weather warm up enough for the whole world of the orchard to reveal itself? She felt like forcing open those closed flowers…Oh, yes, there was a violence in her.

Meanwhile Gil went on: swales, windbreaks, wind and sunlight. The partitioning of the farmstead into zones like the divisions of hell. In the barn he showed her how to feed the ducks, once a day, and don't leave them outside at night again.

"Why not?"

"Raccoons and foxes. They'll dig beneath the wire to get at them."

She looked down at the birds.

"Are there a lot of wild animals around here?"

"Plenty. Raccoons and foxes, as I said, plus coyotes, deer, black bears, owls and rabbits and possums…"

He was inspecting one of the water dispensers, rubbing off some dirt with his thumb.

"Here's an idea, my wife and I could give you manure in exchange for letting the sheep come up and eat the windfall and the locust pods," he said. "Joe used to let us do that."

But she was busy thinking of the animal she was convinced she had killed. Now Gil was trying to unclog dirt from a hole in the dispenser with a twig, though she had the sense he was waiting very carefully for her response.

"All right," she said.

"You can think about it."

"Have you ever killed an animal?" she asked.

Now he stood up and gave her a look she could not decipher.

"A few," he said. "But that's more my wife's business."

"I might have killed an animal."

"When?"

"Driving up. I'm not sure, though."

"Did you see a body?"

"No."

He brushed the dirt from his palms and placed a soft hand on her shoulder.

"You would have known if you'd hit something, sweetie," he said.

They left the barn. Outside the sunshine blinded them.

He turned to her.

"But speaking of animals, Anna, you ought to know we've seen a few black bears this season. They're skittish, shy, easy to scare off, but it wouldn't hurt to be prepared… You ought to drop by my house this week."

A bear. Though his expression had taken on gravity, his plain and friendly voice comforted her. And was he hiding some kind of smile? He removed his hand.

"Anyway, I think I left something in one of the sheds, maybe the greenhouse. Do you mind?"

"Sure."

He went into the greenhouse and emerged three minutes later, shrugging at her from across the grass. He went to check the packing shed. She saw him linger at the tractor near its entrance. He ran his hand along the side of the machine as one might stroke an animal. She wondered if he was reminiscing, not searching, if he was saying goodbye to his friend's things as another way of saying goodbye to his friend, those things which for him were full of meaning and memory, the objects of their friendship and shared labor.

She frowned. She would have liked for the shovels to have been merely shovels.

With a sudden vicious desire for seclusion, she became anxious for him to leave. By the time he began walking back to her, empty-handed and pensive, her smile had faded into a cold and neutral look.

I've got to change the scale of my thinking, she thought dimly. The thought came from beyond her. I've got to think in years, decades.

A mistake could ruin everything. The giant living beast. I should speak slowly, almost imperceptibly, the way a flower blooms unnoticed.

"Find it?"

"No. I must have misremembered."

"What was it?"

He was crossing the grass to get back to her and seemed not to hear. The contours of his thoughts appeared on his face as he approached. His eyes were trailing along the ground.

"I have to get back to the farm," he said. "Remember to drop by."

"Where again?"

"It's right across your property."

They walked west, past the wood fence and a few feet into the woods. There it was down the hill and through the trees: white circles of sheep on grass, large dogs, distant figures, humans and animals. He nodded at her.

"Any afternoon this week," he said. "Keep the wood burning at night or you'll freeze."

Then he went into the thicket, his heavy boots crushing the underbrush.

She watched him go. I should have asked him why he touched the tractor, she thought. I should have told him to back off.

Instead, after drinking coffee, she walked to the end of the driveway and took down the sign that read GADWALL ORCHARD. For her the orchard would be nameless, general, platonic, perfect.

4

After a few days the first green buds of spring like insect eggs were beginning to emerge. The green grays and light pinks of the orchard were birthing deeper and more generous colors in those buds, those buds which to her looked like identical growths stuck to the skeletal limbs of the trees, those buds which seemed to multiply by two or three each day like dividing cells, their centers gesturing at some unknown emerging form, those buds looking like newlyformed clusters of greenish-red birds' eyes. In the mornings she drank coffee and wandered around, looking severely at the trees. The wind was wavy, wobbly, soft on skin. She felt free.

Sometimes, walking through the orchard in this way, she thought she saw branches ripped down from their trees. Trunks engraved with long gorges. Could be claw marks. The invasion of the bear. Squinting at them, conscious of her inexperience, of her inability to distinguish between wreckage wrought by animals and by storms, she tried to map a path of destruction.

It became a nightly ritual to go out into the greenhouse, lean over the garden beds, and, pressing her face up against the glass, look out at the enormous nighttime kingdom of the orchard and wonder if the bear was out there moving. A bear alone in her individuality, she thought dimly, not like the bunnies that freeze when I look at them. She the bear moves like I do, invisible and free. She destroys. She does not move meekly like a semi-sentient extension of plant life, the way field mice and insects move as mere vessels for flowers: she knocks things over and presses her weight into the ground. She embosses herself.

But she doesn't feel guilty like me when she does it. It's part of her being.

Also she wondered what the bear thought of the orchard, of the trees arranged not forestlike but according to the hard logic of agriculture. Could she sense the difference?

Sometimes she was sure it was out there, stalking her like a mother demon. Merciless, dominant, insatiable. Anna's fascination would give way to fear. Her heart would pulse in her neck. She would sprint out of the greenhouse to the cabin, slam the door, breathe hard, then try to sleep, dreaming of the soft black bear pawing around in the windfall in autumn, gentle this time…Spiritually, as in absolution, she would go to sleep granting it her psychic permission: You can eat whatever you like. You're here by night and I by day. You don't bother me like others. You're half a thing of the orchard itself.

And she would wake up again to a new morning, feeling anonymous, undetailed, ambient. She would boil a pot of water. Play at forgetting her own name. Unthinking.

But one of those mornings, five days after her arrival, Anna admitted to herself that something would need to be done. If it really was a bear and not springstorming that destroyed a few new limbs each day.

So why the hesitation? Hadn't he invited her?

Standing on the cabin steps she rolled her wrists.

Something was preventing her from approaching the sheep farm.

When she walked she could see it through the spruce trees, its wide flat pastures, the sheep and goats and gigantic white dogs traversing the grasses like white waves breaking over green oceans. Or sometimes: the odd calm of an empty field. A field so big and bright it looked like a planet. But still. She could not approach. It would be like boarding an enemy spaceship, its flowers grasses and bushes shining with their own strange light like electrical components…If she stumbled through the underbrush that land might open up and swallow her, with the lambs and sheep looking at her dumbly…It was the same when she was driving and saw the other farms and rural houses from her car. Sleepy lights, distant shapes of people strolling through fields of what? Sweet corn and summer squash? Soybeans? She had no idea. The information of the world was smudged. When she drove at night she felt so alone. The night so dark. Everybody else so far away.

It was that she was fearful of breaking her spell of isolation. She continued watching the pastures from her distance. And living alone. She watched how the ewes oriented themselves in the grass, bending down their thick necks to graze, or strolling so slowly from one spot to another that to cross the field could take the light of an entire day. If only I could live with such unconsciousness, she thought. She saw the lambs bend their legs and rest. She saw a goat walk from the enormous gold bales of unrolled hay to the patch of daisies so dotted with flowers it was like a pointillist painting. The smell of musk and smoke and earth on the wind. What was in all those visions? They seemed to pass so slowly. Some days the sheep stood by the fence. Some days they gathered in the center of a field. Watching them Anna would feel a calmness, a calmness that was like a salve. And then: a ram with his stony horns would stride placid and strong across the grass. He with his wide chest would stop at the edge of the pasture to survey beyond the wood fence as though announcing something outside his world. And when it was night Anna would look above the fields at the wreath of the moon and see that it was faintly rainbow, and feel alive and full of gentleness, but then she would look again and see that it was only yellow.

A light anxiety was preceding everything. She was still unsure of how to "work" the orchard. With diligence she searched through Joe's books to supplement what she already knew and what help she could find online, finding in his shelves books by Bill Mollison and Ben Falk and Rosemary Morrow, short and long histories of agriculture, *Developing Your Garden Style*, plenty of books particular to some facet of apple farming, IPM manuals, Joe's budgets and records, a number of historical oddities, including works by ancient agronomists, and dozens and dozens of straightforward, practical, glossy agricultural pamphlets folded in three. There was a book on the woodland colors of the region, unprofessionally bound, likely locally printed. Yes, she looked at the spine: the park service. Some were annotated. His handwriting. Unfamiliar and boxy.

Studying was one of her talents. In the depths of those pages she continued to efface herself, to learn while forgetting, to replace her identity with the facts of her new world. She sat at the office chair and previewed a few of the books, opening one to an early page and reading: *The history of agriculture is the history of deforestation…*

But it didn't feel right at that big desk. It even felt silly. Why? She used to read all evening about the painters of the world, close her eyes and imagine those places, the cosmopolitan cities of Brazil and Spain and Russia… Then it occurred to her that she could read anywhere, in fact should, gone was the sedentary life, she owned a city of trees so why not spread out a little? She could read in the barn across from the rabbits, set up a hammock by the clothesline, clear space on the floor of the greenhouse, sit against the fence and look up at birds. Yes, that's how to learn, she thought brilliantly, putting on her jacket. In the thick of things.

And for instance there were many uses of water: irrigation, habitat, heating, refrigerating, fencing, fire protection, even décor…she spent a whole day just studying water, reading about reintegrating leakage, and that evening she walked through the bamboo thicket where the orange light made the green poles look bronze. She looked at them. Light colors differently from paint, she thought. To paint is to see light, but to see light without painting is something else. Now I am a friend of light and light only. She arrived at the stream. She studied it. She looked around in the soil and thought about how to reroute the water's flow.

Another day she went out to look at the tomato vine in the garden. Greening, unerupted. As dormant as a volcano, maybe soon as red, we'll see, won't we? She tried to laugh with it. She'd learned that tomatoes were a new world crop, here in the global field beside the old world lettuce. How the future was forever cut by fragments of the past, how there was no original ecology, no stasis, how ecological cycles spun imperfectly forward like slow cyclones, not unlike the expanding thrust of galaxies…All there was to aim for was an asymptotic perfection, a harmony that satisfied this moment in ecological history. Flowers for bees. Yes, to approach things asymptotically, until the space between the orchard and idyllic perfection, a kind of undiluted ecology born from minerals she wanted to believe existed, with its primordial or Jurassic megaflora, could be almost touched with the tip of a finger. Right?

Right.

That night, returning a book to the shelf, she encountered the drawing.

It was pinned, alongside other papers and photographs, to the corkboard on the wall behind the computer monitor.

She recognized it as a sketch she'd done at twenty, almost a decade ago now. It was from her studies of aspen forests. She touched it. It was drawn on the thick, beige paper of her early sketchbooks. At that time she'd wanted to make huge, zoomed-in paintings of flora and fauna so close up they could hardly be recognized, warping them into other things, defamiliarizing them with bold colors, unnaturally vivid, almost neon. She had liked the heightened way of looking at the world of the impressionists, symbolists, luminists, and watercolorists, but wanted to transform that foggy, delicate quality into something like an onslaught, into cannons of hard perception, and though she'd tried to articulate her paintings as mixing artifice with landscape painting—"the colors of screens and club lights and advertisements and candy wrappers"—the truth was that she simply liked to engulf herself in color, pure blue, pure green, painting so close up to the easel that the edges of the world disappeared. She did not like articulating. At any rate the paintings looked gaudy. And she really had no sense of how to announce her work to the world, so they said, so she had painted less and less frequently until she stopped altogether.

No great tragedy, people peter out. You annihilate the shameful parts of yourself, forget your failures, you're born again. Besides, how horribly anyone had understood—as if her desire to make work had had anything to do with public success.

So what to do now?

Live a painting, for one, instead of making them. Closer to what I meant anyway, she thought bitterly. And that kind of progress will be unmeasurable.

For two, destroy the sketch. Its existence is a stain on the new one.

She snatched the paper off the wall and ripped it down the middle. Nice tearing sound.

But even after throwing the scraps away their presence continued needling at her. She slept poorly. In the morning she fished them out of the trash, agitated. There could be no more waiting, she decided, she had done enough studying, after all it had been over a week, the weather warming and so on. It was nearly April. It was necessary to construct a new relationship with creation. Don't be shy, she told herself, it's true. Don't be shy. She stuffed the scraps of paper in her jacket pocket and drove into town, passing the other farms with their huge metallic machines, the reapers and balers hanging still and menacing like gods sleeping in guardian statues. She threw the scraps into the first public dumpster she found. She contemplated the dumpster's blue.

By the time she arrived at the nursery her first act on the orchard was fullformed in her mind: it would be a sacrifice or an offering. Inside people were touching seeds and bulbs and bushes. With an uncertain heart she considered the apple saplings. Rootstocks, scionwood, sleeping eyes. Her first act would have to be complex, but not too far beyond her abilities. Symbolic, but not meaningless. She settled on a dwarf rootstock whose tag read "hardy and well-anchored—resistant to collar rot but vulnerable to fireblight." She bought scionwood from a cultivar called *Alice*, a thin rod of wood that promised sweet mild fruit. Her first act would be a transference, the mutant creation of a little tree, a little tree like a little girl, small and almost sickly, limp and slightly gray, something like herself, something defenseless and frail she could heal beneath her hands, her own two hands…She held the rootstock in her hands. Just like a parent holds a child. She checked out.

Cradling the little beings she drove home and brought them to the end of one of the Teratourgima rows. She dug deep into the earth with a shovel, as close to the row as she could while remaining in undiluted sunlight. The ground was hard. The work was difficult. Twice she returned to the cabin to catch her breath, drink water, and try to watch the same grafting video over and over again, waiting with mute frustration for the video to buffer…she studied and deciphered the same three diagrams. Or else, as a means of rest, she walked down the rows of trees with a handheld bottle of miscible oil from the shed, spraying them, investigating their roots, pretending to map out where to lay the next compost. She touched the branches with intimacy. She kept digging. When she had produced a hole like a grave she lowered the root system shallowly into the ground. She put the dirt back, the grass. Pushing the grass atop the hole she felt like a deity, a deity who terraforms the world. Kneeling before the rootstock she held the limp scion in her hand like a grass rosary. The tiny thing shivering in the wind, like me. The new thing, like me. She understood it the kind way we understand others: how it would grow just as animals grow. She was trying to collapse everything into one thing. Quivering she was struggling to arrive at her position as a priestess. Meditating she understood the questions of fate and intention to be vanishing, the past erasing itself finally, the future blank and beautiful: how the present with its harsh wind and blinding light dominates the future and the past. Things were happening plainly in front of her. The gentleness. Cutting the rootstock and the scion identically with her knife she felt as though she were cutting herself loose from something, what?…she fit the scion and the stock together, looking for the right spot. She had a violent vision of the ocean, kneeling before the rootstock she imagined herself kneeling on the white sands before some ocean, facing the ocean with its red sun, which was at once the grass, the line of trees, the orchard sky. The love she was trying to summon subsumed the image of the little tree, the little mutt in the dirt. The little twig: easy, traitorous, serene. My new happiness will advance like an ocean, reaching out its broad hands like tidal waves out to destroy whatever contradicts it, swallowing my weaknesses, continents, even, I'll be subsumed into the immensity of the orchard, infinite from where I sit kneeling on the ground with this little scion, birds skimming along the tops of the fruit trees like liquid over a surface, finally above, dark bells, divine perches, a new kind of divinity that faces the clouds instead of descending from them: my orchard as my little shrine: the scion, its first offering: not a church or even a celestial terrace but a shrine with incense, idols, children, tealight candles. A simplicity mirroring vastness. Seas between one tree and another. She stood up, satisfied. The new growth was affixed to the row like its tiara. It was late afternoon and she was tired. She breathed.

    Suddenly her eyes hurt. The dirt was stinging her fingernails. She felt hot.

The farm was silent back at her.

It was one of several failures. But I'm getting closer, she reassured herself. Try to feel a pleasure in failing but getting closer, she reassured herself, generously this time. There's no one here to see you.

"Say hello," she instructed the other trees. Besides the clerk at the nursery, it had been days since she'd spoken to another person.

She went inside. Yes, it was hard work. Her muscles would get sore and sorer. Sore? No, they'll burn with the pleasure of a joy, they'll brush by joy. Yes, that's better: like a purifying fire. She thought the phrase slowly, "purifying fire," etching it onto her brain. She went inside to make dinner, trying to smile, etching it. She ran herself a hot bath, watched the foam bubble up, trying to smile, etching it. In the bath she moved her soft limbs through the water, feeling the fresh ache begin to subside a little, and disappearing down into the bubbles, effacing herself, miming drowning, she warmed her feet at the edge of the enamel in the dry radiance of the serenely humming water heater.

5

Her failure made her feel weak, human. She was looking for the right way to interface with those trees, since sometimes, living hermetically beside them, she glimpsed a brief beam of something enormous and iridescent just before it vanished...how to capture it? And at the same time a new kind of loneliness was arriving alongside the burning of her muscles, weighing like a person's hand in the center of her chest, and she was beginning to question her capacity to really adjust to complete solitude. She took photos of the farmstead—why? Just to prove she was there. Not to anyone else. She deleted every message, declined every call. She recorded a cat blinking slowly at the camera with its bubblecrystal eyes, the cat looking into the phone then squirming away under the porch as Anna stepped forward zooming in with two fingers, clumsy, turning on the flash to capture the cat crouching over kittens in the shade, seeing the tapetum glow back at her from the minerals in the cat's eyes, minerals in the eyes as in the earth, and why couldn't she rewire her origin to become part of the earth here too, like the cat who was born here and would die here? Redeye is red because of blood, she remembered. Nothing was alleviated.

Against her better judgment, in those days of confused fragility, she called her mother.

It was in the afternoon. They had opted to video chat. Her mother's image lagged on the screen. She kept freezing in front of the empty wine bottles, unwashed dishes, filth.

"Well? How are you adjusting?" came the voice, emulsified by the poor connection.

"It's beautiful here."

"Give me a tour! The curtains look different."

"I'm on a desktop," said Anna. "And I haven't done anything to the curtains."

"Oh."

It was an old computer with a bulbous monitor, like a bubble, like the cat's eyes. Though the image was blurry, she could see the unfocused dead look in her mother's face, sense the desolation of the rest of her apartment.

"I'll take a video and send it to you."

"Great."

Her mother smiled at something off-screen, then returned to Anna and frowned again. The sunshine glared over her image like a net of light. Anna adjusted the curtains. They sat together in miserable silence.

"Have you met any of your neighbors?"

Anna pretended not to hear.

"Anna? I said have you met anyone?"

"A friend of his came over. He said to stop by."

"Have you?" The voice was completely disembodied.

"Not yet."

"Why not? Go visit!"

She promised vaguely that she would.

"Anyone else?"

"No."

The screen flooded red. Then came chopped-up siren sounds. Her lagging face stayed blank. But blankness did not faze Anna.

"What are you doing out there? Honestly."

The filth of the apartment was stranger. Her mother had always been a clean woman. Was that grief? Anna thought. Should I be deadeyed and crying too? I never even think about it. I can't imagine a place like this living so vile.

Anna didn't answer. She imagined what it would be like to do what her mother wanted, to abandon the orchard to move home, or at least to visit, the cobwebs reconstructing themselves, the newlyliving greenhouse plants withering, the summer bugs invading the trees…

"Call me once you're done dallying. We'll get it on the market and you can come back to your life," her mother said before hanging up.

She turned the computer off. It was quiet again.

She felt strangely comforted. Loved a little. Sad too: or like a vessel emptied of liquid.

She spent a few minutes staring at the rug, trying to untangle those emotions. The colors of the world seemed overexposed, grainy. Her head hurt.

One sweet thing to this anonymity, she thought, to the nonsentience of these plants and animals: nobody passes judgment if I'm feeling lonely, nobody's here to pity me. I can be full of rage in a silent world. It's a different thing to be alone out in public in front of everybody, all the windows of the world looking down on a solitude as shameful as it is agonizing. The spectacular solitude of life-near-others.

This solitude is sweeter, gentler, deeper.

Then she felt angry with herself, since some internal movement was still trying to drag her back into the world. Why had she called her mother?

She stepped outside. Sound touched her like a balm. Little birds, so sweet on the ear. She saw them in the bushes. Little brown birds. Sparrows? Maybe some type of sparrow. And the bush was a buckthorn bush. She had learned. Here was a world that no longer appeared as a tangled and undecipherable wall of green, but as…the sparrows in the buckthorn.

Transporting her image outside the farmstead like that, revealing it to her mother...

Better for all of us to do as we've always done and retreat into our private graves.

But there was still a kind of tranquility. She exhaled. She went to mount the tractor, which she rode like a blue mechanical horse through the tall grasses of the orchard, hosing the first trees down with neem oil as though baptizing them.

I will gather up the courage to approach that paradise of beasts, she thought. Yes.

Afraid of trapezing through the underbrush like Gil she drove her car around the enormous block—a block of field and fruit, vegetables, metal machines, and so on—to the sheep farm. It was morning. She drove through the gates and saw the empty fields of plain green grass. Then livestock began slowly dotting her field of vision, sheep and goats, some snug with blue and green fleeces over their wool; some isolated, some congealed like sticky rice. Dogs too. Black and white herding dogs, the colossal white dogs she'd seen from afar, a terrier...One by one they peeled off from their pastures to run and bark happily beside her car. She was scared to hit them. She slowed her car to a crawl. A squat shingled house painted green formed at the end of the dirt road, and when she parked and exited, the whirlpool of dogs revolved around her and she laughed and stroked them and stumbled with their legs until Gil opened the door with a face as red and joyous as a cherub's.

Inside they sat in plastic chairs around a large square table. It was dim. The television was on and dirt was scattered by the front and back door. Gil looked at her with bewildered happiness, as though afraid to speak.

"I was beginning to think you'd gotten lost!" he said finally.

"Just settling in," said Anna. She tried to smile.

Gil sniffed and nodded. He took a pair of glasses out of his shirt pocket, put them on, then looked again at Anna. His magnified eyes looked big and squirrely. He took his cell phone out of his pants pocket and quickly stood back up.

"Let me just phone my wife to tell her that you're here," he said.

He walked into the kitchen.

She looked around. The stream of sound from the television was tinny…it was only the weather channel, but the unpleasant whine from the speakers was forcing itself…she felt the ghost of a headache. The place was filled with…paper towels stacked up in corners, plastic wrappers from packages, the trash needed to be taken out, a vacuum cleaner stood grimy and omniscient by the door…cluttered, a bit dismal. There were rugs on the floor, blankets on the couch, unwashed dishes…She became aware of her face. She was frowning.

"Anna, coffee?" Gil called.

"Yes, thank you."

She heard him pour water. She heard the gas stove ignite. The woman on the weather channel made huge windmills with her hands as she spoke. Gil returned.

"She's on her way," he said. "And how are you? How's the orchard? Any big changes?"

He lingered on the final word.

Anna froze. *Has he been watching me?*

No, of course not: changes are what one makes. Still, she knew she did not want to tell him a thing. Her psychic interface with the apple trees, the baby buds, the moving waterfeathers of the ducks…

Gil grunted and shifted in his chair.

"It's all right if not, like you said, you're just settling in. See some bears?"

"I think so."

"You think so?"

"I think I heard one out there."

Gil looked at her with those gigantic and curious eyes.

"Were you scared?" he whispered.

She was about to answer when the back door banged open. A woman with dark heavy long hair came into the kitchen. She shook dirt from her boots and brushed grass and straw off her pants. She looked almost as sunbaked as Gil, prematurely wrinkled, and she was such an enormous, broad-shouldered woman that Anna thought she must be wearing heeled boots or a shoulder-padded jacket or some other magnifying garment, but as she took them both off, her boots and her jacket, looking expressionless as one of the stony rams, Anna saw that she was not. It was Tamara.

Tamara glanced into the kitchen.

"You left the whistle open," she said hoarsely.

Gil looked at Anna, playfully rolled his eyes.

"I know. Tamara, this is Anna," he said.

"You told me, Joe's grandkid. The painter."

Tamara went into the kitchen, then returned with three mugs. She blew on her coffee and didn't sit down.

"How's it going?" Gil asked her.

"Not yet," said Tamara. "I'll go back out there in a second."

"One of our ewes is about to lamb," Gil said to Anna.

Tamara looked at Anna too, with intensity and a bit of evil pleasure. Anna squirmed and took a sip of her coffee. She lowered her mug and the woman was still looking at her.

"So you're going to paint here?" asked Tamara. "Paint the countryside?"

"I don't think so."

"Good. You won't have time. Then what will you do?"

Anna considered what Tamara would want to hear. Her throat felt tight.

"Just work on the farm," she said finally.

"Good."

Everybody was drinking their coffee fast. Something in that woman's tone made Anna shiver. She hadn't stopped looking at Anna with that dark and amused expression.

Anna did not see the rigidity that was forming between Gil and Tamara. She was looking out the window at the meadow, instinctively fleeing Tamara's gaze, trying to see if she could glimpse her own farm through the trees like she could see theirs from hers.

But she saw nothing. Green mass of leaves. Totally opaque.

"Um," she said without turning her head. "I'm all right, though. I like being surrounded by plants and animals."

"Good," Gil said. "Hopefully it won't get too monotonous!"

That last word rang out again. Well, how to get at this sideways, Anna thought.

She looked at Gil, who had finished his drink and was now smudging some of the coffee stain from his mug to lick it off his finger.

Monotony…she envisioned it: the repeated motion of twisting the black stem of an apple off its tree, five hours with an ax in her hand halving dry logs of firewood while hearing the dull metal thud. Then piling up the logs and looking at their hundreds of gently brown rings, staring back at her like the steady eyes of animals. She wasn't looking for adventure, how to explain? How to get at it sideways. Hopefully that wasn't what Tamara thought. She was looking for a certain absolute stillness of psyche, branches like extensions of her fingers, roots like blood vessels. To build up a world from a few repeated actions.

"I don't really mind being bored or finding things 'monotonous,'" she tried to articulate. "I just want to get closer to a certain way of being."

In fact, she thought, suddenly smiling, to act otherwise implied a certain absence of grace. Suddenly she felt very calm.

"That feeling of 'monotony'—that's what I want. That's what I'm after."

She glanced at them. They were looking at her wordlessly.

Faltering slightly, she tried to speak more to Gil than to Tamara.

"I want to feel the depth of pleasure in the orchard's slow changes."

Already feeling uncertain and incoherent, Anna began gripping her mug. "I want to feel that 'monotony' down to my bones. Do you get what I mean?"

Gil looked sensitively down at the wood of the table, his chin in his palm.

Meanwhile Tamara's disgust had spread across her face like a poison.

The woman on the weather channel droned on and on.

Anna tried to fold her impulse neatly back into squares. Tuck it away in some corner of her body. No coming back from this. Run away? There's the door.

Gil lifted his hat and ran his hand over his thinning hair.

Tamara lifted her mug. She took a sip. Her sip had the cold elegance of a ballerina.

"Time to head back out," said Tamara. "Why don't you come along, Anna? I think it might do you good."

She trailed behind them through the bluegreen day. She walked sullenly, because she didn't quite understand what she had said wrong…Wasn't it good she felt attuned to this life?

In the lambing pen a pinkfaced ewe lay contracting in the straw. She was extremely fat and her engorged belly was red like an exploding garnet. Gil bent down to feel her breathing, then they all waited for twenty or so minutes while Gil talked about the flock, the Merinos and the East Fresians, the dairy co-op, his favorite ewes, butter. Eventually the ewe tried to stand, Gil snapped latex gloves over his hands, and a bubble began to inflate from the ewe's backside. A revolting yellow color. All the while Gil was speaking cheerfully. He squatted and watched the ewe. Tamara watched the ewe but she also watched Anna. Anna tried to watch. Anna tried not to vomit. Within the yellow a muted iron color was emerging, like the sheep was laying a stone egg, a painfully enormous metallic apple…she weakly bleated. She contracted again.

Gil reached inside the animal and tugged on something, still chatting, about what Anna couldn't even say, she was just trying to suppress a gag, and the metallic apple was revealed as hooves attached to weak little legs that Gil yanked out like a pair of amberdrenched branches. He tore out the whole lamb.

The lamb was like a disgusting dark swamp of fluid.

Gil shook it by its baby face and dragged it around the front of the ewe, who began to lick it.

"That's an easy one," Tamara said. "You get used to it."

Anna felt her face: it was contorted with repulsion. She tried to calm it, to look coolly interested. But Tamara had already seen.

"You know, we're only guaranteed a profit on about a third of the ewes," she said slowly. "Whenever we aren't lambing, I work part-time at the slaughterhouse to make ends meet. I get up at three each morning to take care of someone else's animals, all crowded in filthy pens, animals that live and die in darkness so that ours can live in sunlight. It's borrowed happiness. You're luckier. Working in crops, you don't have these problems. Different problems, maybe. But there's no money in lounging around, overlooking the pastures, dreaming of the passage of time, contemplating how the woods affect your soul."

Anna looked at her. A slaughterhouse job...but she saw the repetition of its pigs like crops, identical, mutated, bred to odd sizes. The animal made plastic. So that's what this is about? Hard to imagine a place like that, it was true.

Also hard to imagine a woman like that existing alongside Gil.

Gil glanced apologetically up at the two of them.

"Another one's coming," he said quietly.

Tamara looked down at him and as their eyes met both seemed to soften as much as stiff bodies could: like hardwood turning into softwood.

And now that she was free from her gaze, Anna was able to think: so they hadn't understood.

I'm not afraid of cruelty, she thought. I'm not.

She made a point of crouching by Gil.

"I'll help you with this one."

"All right," he said. "I'll tell you where to pull."

But this lamb was arriving with more difficulty. The yellow orb burst early, not that Anna even knew what that meant, but the ewe was heaving and making sounds of pain. Anna studied it. There's the lamb's hooves and nose again, as though eager to descend into the ocean of the world. Or just one hoof? Just one hoof. She reached out her hand but Gil gently intercepted it and said it would be better if he handled this one. He reached in. Seemed to rearrange the baby in the birth canal. Anna thought: Not even born and already the world touches you. Gil pulled out the lamb. There was a lot of blood on the back of its legs.

She steeled her stomach. After all, all it is is a pretty pool of colors, right? Ochre and crimson and violet.

Without a word she took the lamb's face in her hand and shook it as Gil had done.

She stared at Tamara as she did so. Tamara returned her gaze.

That's right, Anna thought, though she was also afraid. This is my world too. I'll interface with it on my terms. You won't bully me out of it.

"Give him another shake," she heard Gil say. "He hasn't breathed yet."

Still looking at Tamara Anna shook its face again. Tamara was still looking too. They remained. Finally Tamara's look weakened and her eyes dropped.

"You're hurting it," she said quietly.

Anna looked back at the lamb. Its little eyes were squinting under her grip. It was shaking its head like it barely knew how. Gil removed Anna's hand and shook the lamb a bit differently. Finally it moved its head on its own and the mother came around to clean it.

Back in the house Gil brewed more coffee. Everyone washed their hands and stood around the kitchen, looking for a way to restore some fragment of harmony.

Gil brought up the bear.

"Right," said Tamara. "Greg's wife told me they shot at one the other day but missed. It fled north."

"That's towards us," Gil told Anna. "Poor thing."

"There really was no need."

Tamara's eyes drifted to Anna.

Anna was looking at her coffee. Prideful, guilty.

"But I don't think it would have come around if they'd had some dogs," Tamara said.

"Dogs?" said Anna.

"I'm thinking of livestock guardians, though people use them for land in general. We breed and use them." She pretended to inspect her mug. "Gil suggested you take two."

"Careful she doesn't gouge you! She sells them for four hundred a pup," Gil interjected. "Some family."

Tamara smiled thinly.

"No, we were going to give some of Toby's litter to Joe anyway," she said. "They're Anatolian-Pyrenees mixes. Great dogs."

Anna blinked. Tamara really did have enough severe clarity for the two of them. She spoke so quickly, so precisely. Something in her voice was airier now, like earth on wind.

"You're giving me dogs?"

"Gil didn't say?"

"No."

"I meant to surprise her," Gil said.

"It's good you like animals. There's a particular happiness in keeping dogs. Ducks and rabbits are fine, even sheep, but there's something else in the company of a farm dog. You'll see."

"Sometimes at night they'll all howl together and we'll join on in with them. Won't we, Tamara?"

He gave a little howl and Tamara smacked him lightly. Anna laughed. The three of them went out again to one of the sheds. The sun touched everything, the gloomy greenblue cut with new yellow. In the shed, a few young dogs were dozing in the hay and they raised their sleepy heads as the door opened. They must have been about six or seven months old, if Anna could guess, their brown eyes large and intelligent, illuminated, seeking something…they were dirty like wild animals. But unlike the lambs seeped in color, the dogs were pale like doves. Anna crouched down, rubbed a floppy ear with her finger. Good girl. Their little teeth. She smiled.

Still kneeling, she turned around to thank them, but silhouetted by the doorway light she saw that Tamara was relaying something quietly to Gil.

Gil started to say something, stopped, then tried again. Inaudible.

Anna turned back to the puppies.

Already they were spooling out happiness, already they seemed to hold the promise of alleviating the secret corrupting loneliness. It was what she needed. An inhuman companionship.

She chose a large female white puppy with fur like a king's stoat mantle and a silly-looking male with big brown patches over his eyes. She named them without even standing, choosing the first two syllables that came to mind: Midge and Pell. So christened were the dogs.

"See you soon, I hope," Gil said as they loaded the animals into Anna's car.

"She'll need help training them," said Tamara, "so she'll have to."

Anna nodded, waved, and departed with the dogs. As she drove away she felt her body saturate with melancholy. There's no sense hoping for another psychic erasure, she thought. I'll have to live with the ambivalent impression I've made on other people. She gripped the steering wheel again, pensive, stern. Then she glanced at the dogs in the rearview. They were climbing over each other, tongues lolling, hanging their heads out the half-open window and blinking their tiny eyes in the rough wind. She drove home. And after working all the next day, she lay down on the porch of the cabin and listened for the dogs probing around in the grass. She called them so she could stroke them as the sun set. They came one after the other, and sometimes from the nearby pasture they heard the other dogs bark.

6

As the weather warmed and the greens grew greener Anna understood she would need to do everything in her power to attain that unconscious feverstate she'd glimpsed twice but been unable to wholly capture. If she didn't incorporate herself, she would lose herself completely: she would stumble back into death, the dull world. Or: better to say she was already lost, that she had lost herself deliberately, like a snake shedding its skin, and that the only path left was to finish decomposing that fragile shell of self into the earth, free herself from human suffering, live as the extension of something insentient, inhuman, serene. She had to destroy what was left of her identity. She began by moving her painting equipment, which she'd left ambivalently in the corner of the living room as though some quiet afternoon she might pick it up again, to the wood cabinet in the back of the hothouse. She pressed the black mop brush against her cheek so the soft hairs fanned out cold almost wet against her face, a sensation she'd always loved, before bidding it farewell forever.

As she did, she thought of how she'd once read that in orchards plagued by smog the pollution was so bad all the honeybees had died and the farmhands pollinated the apple trees with paintbrushes. They carried huge bags of pollen in one arm against their bodies, dipped those pollenbrushes intimately into the apple flowers. Another life. It could have been me. But here the skies were blue, the sunsets pale and mild, the stars oddly plentiful. She could see stars! And the bees were just swimming through the air. Approaching a milkweed flower one day she even reached out one of her own fingers to stroke the striped velvet veil of a honeybee. It reminded her of the rose bush right up against her front door when she was a kid, she'd always felt so scared leaving the house next to all those insects swarming around like clouds of electrons...so scared...once or twice they'd even stung her. Will this one? It didn't. It would have been all right. And even though part of her almost wanted to destroy the beehive, when she eventually found one in a row of trees deep within the orchard, with all its one hundred thousand repeating honeycomb cells in the branches of a tree heavy with white blossoms, like a fractured citrine in a sea of pearls...she didn't.

That was all good and pleasant, but it wasn't thoughtless. She could stroke the honeybee and think. Walking around the orchard wouldn't be enough. She was going to forget everything except: it's spring, the vegetables are growing in the garden, apple flowers bloom, days flow.

She would need to experience the origin moment. To go back to the very beginning. Agriculture, it seemed, was a decisive moment in human history, the moment they distinguished themselves from animals, so could something within it allow her to peer over the precipice of the human? Somewhere into that lost unconsciousness. Then happiness would expand frankly and inanimately, like the bold unfurling of a flag. Sometimes the idea of that unconsciousness scared her, looking out at all the flowering trees, young birds taking off from branches, flower spiders immobile on the petal: and the orchard was something so large and complex you couldn't even see it in a single look...how could she turn that fear into deference? All she could ever take in was the orchard partly viewed. The branches forming vertical triangles between their rows, the almost insufferable brightness of the sun which matured the apple buds, which exploded the flowers out of their pod…Not knowing what happened in the orchard at all moments, she could imagine it contained secret processes, like a mirage island always out of reach: like within it was some ancient colossal being, its limbs weighed down by apples and by vines…fantastical things, childhood fantasies. Invisible spindles, ghosts, crystalline structures. The cyclic forest of fruit. Unknowing was the first step to unconsciousness.

To experience the origin moment she would have to rebuild the world. It would be a daily psychic task. After rewinding past the beginning of humanity she would be able to see the orchard like a primeval animal. No, she thought, farther back. I want to see it on geologic scales of time, the very beginning, rocks and lightning, fire, space, a million years of rain. The gradual pounding of rock into dirt, everything that prefigured the invention of agriculture in the first place.

One of those moments must be the moment life became so unbearable. Whether it was human life or life itself she didn't know. She would have to search all along the timeline. Back before life was death. Life could not be so unbearable at its core.

She tried spending long stretches of time standing in the fields. She counted each leaf on the trees until the numbers stopped making sense, or traced the varied ways their trunks curved upwards towards the clouds. And then she tried to content herself with simply looking. Green. Blue. Movement. Stillness. Sun. Don't think at all.

Sometimes at night she missed the warmth of another person. She lay in bed and tried to eviscerate the thought. She did not forgive herself these feelings. She chastised herself like penance.

In the morning she would try again. It would take practice. She perceived with immense effort. She noticed more, thought less. Spinach, lettuce, radish, and rainbow chard sprouted up beside the kitchen. Green heads bursting like hatchlings out of black soil. Dogs now, finally sunshowers, and me, Anna, I tend the orchard. I look at things for hours. Every day the old world recedes and I live more and more in the perfect present. Isn't that right? She opened the windows. The wind flowed through the house. Light and shadow moved with time. She stood up straighter, loose and muscular. What day was it again?

Loneliness continued to threaten her. She could not succumb to it. She had to feel it and endure. She tried to pass entire days without thinking a single human word, especially not words of bodies, flesh, affection. Instead she sculpted her thoughts into shapes, colors, images, sounds, abstractions. She suspended psychic barriers over language like clouds over the sun. In proportion to each word she smothered, she felt something expand in the ribcage. "I'm getting closer," she'd think after these exercises. She'd try not to think it next time.

In the fullest moments she was able to pass hours with nothing inside but her concentration on the repeated rhythm of the hand. Emptiness, emptiness. She laid out straw in a circle around the trunk of a tree, beginning at the six and rotating clockwise until the straw fanned out in a goldthread circle to sequester water and smother weeds…or she weeded by grabbing a handful of the malignant grass at its base, twisting it, and yanking until she heard the pleasant snapping sound. She removed it from the earth, deposited the corpse of the plant into her black bucket. The earth in her hands: wet, pliant, fragrant. Kind of cold. Nothing but a pink wash of color in her head, vast, misty, pale, sparkling, a murmuring soundlessness moving around in her brain like something-celestial, lush shimmering sounds…all her senses getting mixed together…she was soon able to pass entire days like this, and at night, before bed, almost intoxicated by the beauty of the days green gold and pink: she thought of no one and petted the dogs.

Because the dogs were saving her from the necessity of other people.

Tamara had been right. They were just right. They were growing each week, bounding into things. And since they'd started guarding the orchard, it had been undisturbed like a holy temple garden. The dogs ran around or lay in clover patches with their big tongues lolling out and their eyes bright and happy and their brains not thinking, just looking and protecting like Anna wanted to do. Seeing those brown eyes reflected in her own was teaching her about nonverbal love, and how to extend that alien empathy to the ducks, the rabbits, of course the plants, the cats? The animals she knew less intimately but was beginning to apprehend, yes, she was beginning to love even the beings which feared her. And soon that distance will be obliterated. She held her hand out gently to the rabbit, watched its muscles relax and its heart still. Sometimes one touched its nose to her finger. Was it smiling?

Animals, like bark, she discovered, could be distinguished by their textures. The honeybees had their striped velvet, the fur of the dogs was thick and watery, the rabbits were so soft so gray so silky, the ducks hid beneath those thousands of feathers like hundreds of sandy threads fanning out from hollow stems. Like petrified ferns. She was tempted to give them all names, but knew the broadness of the life she was cultivating resisted anthropomorphization. At times she even regretted naming the dogs. But no, the dogs were different. Half-human. They're my bridge to the new world.

But then how did the animals relate to each other? Sounds, scents, colors? How do plants relate to animals, minerals to plants, water to minerals? Like she had done with her own thinking she abstracted the names of the animals into sounds, pure sounds, so that their calling-notes were nonsymbolic and nonreferential…Better, she could identify the rabbits purely by the shapes and colors in her mind's eye as she stroked them. This one: quick yellow-green lines radiate out from a single point above his left eye. Spinning, energetic. Another: a dull, blue, pulsing rhythm, sometimes grayish and swirling like fog, from deep within the rabbit's pelvis. The last: a slow, churning, incandescent red, a color she could feel very deep inside her almost pressing against the muscley chambers of a heart…

She was righting the world like a flower watered. She was making things comprehensible.

Bitterly she reflected how for so long she had tried mechanically, arduously to find a way to live like this, walking around the parks near her apartments, reading beautiful books, watching beautiful films, trying to make meaningful conversation, meaningful connections with the people around her, but after everything passed through her she was always left feeling dead, unaffected, and with a nothingness that was even worse than suffering…now she was really doing it…"rapture" was becoming so indistinguishable from "life," she couldn't help but cry from happiness sometimes while lying in the grass corridor between two apple rows. A bright happy emptiness. Not a dark one. She would lie there and then a warm breeze would arrive…and the breeze would be warm.

She'd wanted so badly to be happy, and now from the earth she watched the breeze move above her through the trees. It snaked through the branches like some divinely invisible beast muscling through leaves. She learned to see how wind moved through the orchard. Its swales and windbreaks like canals. How a well-placed tree could interrupt whole rivers of wind. And whenever the breeze reached her she felt her body reduce itself to something purely organic. Purely material.

It occurred to her that the things happening to her were part of two large arcs: her own and the arc of humanity. In her arc, she had arrived at the part of life where unadulterated happiness is discovered and you try as hard as you can to carry it through to your death. She had pinned it down and her life would end here and end slowly: a long half-century, hopefully, of bliss-tremors. The deadness of life made vibrant. Yes: in a place like this one can even look forward to death.

In the larger arc, she was one of those few lucky people who had discovered the secret.

The secret was that there were many ways to live, but only a few which lifted one from the pit of misery into something like a transcendence. What they all had in common was the annihilation of the self, the submission to something outside the bounds of time.

Believing this, she gained the ability to keep the holy secret of the orchard in her heart wherever she went. She walked with the dogs through dells, vales, forests, and groves around the orchard, across the river to the north with its fast liquid pastures moving ceaselessly through the woods, watching it with her dogs for the arcs of bass and rainbow trout which Midge always lunged at, her teeth snapping at the beads of water left like comet tails by those little sparkling fish… They would pass flowers whose names Anna had not yet learned, and which, like a child, she devised her own names for, and which the more docile Pell was always trying to gnaw on: six-petaled broad wheelflower, blue star cluster, drooping redbell… Anna didn't want to know their "true" names. And finally, coming home from their walks in the late light, she gathered the dandelion and chamomile that grew beside the cabin steps and the stinging nettle that lined the packing shed for an herbal tea. She mixed it with lemon and with honey from the glass jar the ants were always invading. (She scooped the ants out.) And after boiling the herbs in a kettle she would let a few of those limp chamomile blossoms float like water lilies in the brew, softly touching her lips as she sipped: the closest she would ever come again to romance.

Afterward, placing the empty mug in the sink, she was able to sleep a night with no fear, no sadness, no longing, nothing.

And then she worked.

She spent days hosing down the trees with the backpack sprayer and stoically harvesting the new bamboo. Since she'd hardly touched the bamboo since arriving, it was hard work. She had to plunge her shovel deep into the dirt and gravel to remove the nests of roots. And then like a fairy prince she trekked into the glowing green thicket with her lopper and her hacksaw and struck the ligaments of the bamboo as though slaying them. Sometimes the older stocks would shake loose white lichen when struck, and parasites would fall out of the culm and scuttle off. She went on. Colors told her which stalks were ripe for harvest. Some were so fresh and glossy they looked plastic. Some she felled for shoots, others for timber. Afterward she loaded the poles onto the utility trailer, looked back at the stumplike nodes across the grass, wiped the sweat from her brow, sighed.

She was trying to think of herself not as the owner of the orchard but as a kind of sentinel. The wholeness of the orchard confronted her repetitively, daily. The apple rows, the deliberate spiral of the garden, and the perfect orientation of the bamboo in its grove, with the vivax up front and the guadua behind. All these environments had been designed by another hand, the hand of the relative…and its smaller details designed by the orchard's secret laborers, whose names she would never know. The blackberry bushes appearing spontaneously between two rows, planted by a bird…the degree to which water pooled in the watercress…the precise matrix of cross-pollinations. Humbly Anna extracted and facilitated. Like the unlearned process of painting, she observed and dutifully she reacted.

So she hoped.

The days kept passing. May finished its first week. May deepened. Early crickets appeared in the evening grass. And on a windy night Anna recognized again the movements of the bear.

It was here!

While washing the dishes she thought she heard its moaning. The shadows of its blocky body in the dark windows. The dogs were inside. Pell with his high voice was barking at the night.

Anna stormed over to the wood door and thrust it open.

"Hey!" she called out.

The winds blew. They carried away her voice. Standing in the doorway she squinted into the darkness, tried to see from an impossible angle over the black hill to the black fruit trees. Nothing. Had the bear heard her? Had she scared it off?

Then both dogs flew out of the cabin.

They ran off into the void. Was the bear looking in their direction? Was it coming or was it fleeing? She imagined those coal-colored lips stained with berry juice, the salmon pink of a tongue-between-fangs…Tiny brown ferocious eyes, just a little nervous look beneath those round ears…How she'd right herself clumsily with on those four heavy paws as the dogs approached. The dogs were barking distantly now, their voices drowning in the wind. Anna smelled dew, darkness, growing fruit, night flowers. To the bear, she thought, slow, serene, frozen, dumbstruck: it's only that I have to do this and at least I'm not destroying you. Things are changing. Then fear caught up to her. The bear with its immensity. No, black bears are small, it's mostly harmless. She's gentle and startled. Anna struggled to hear the increasingly distant sound of the dogs.

The dogs stopped barking.

The wind was blowing hard.

Anna waited by the door, afraid to call out.

She heard the ambiguous sound of movement.

Then Midge ran up the steps and back inside, pausing briefly to lick Anna's right hand. Twenty seconds passed. Then Pell scooted in behind her. The dogs seemed cheerful, unscathed, panting, their bodies fluttering with happiness at their midnight sprint. Anna closed the door. The dogs flopped down. Sometimes they returned to the window to gaze seriously out at the blackness of the farmstead.

Slowly Anna bent down and took Midge's face in her hands, stared into those eyes, tried to discern something. Happy to be outside? Or just to be useful? Midge squirmed away.

In the morning she found what looked like the bear's heart-shaped pawmarks smeared in the dark spring mud near a row of Teratourgima apples.

That's right, the bear was out there. But I reacted instinctually,

Anna thought with triumph. The three of us did. We felt and did not think.

Neither did she think whenever Tamara came by to help train the dogs. She merely obeyed as though she were herself being trained. She watched as Tamara introduced them to the ducks, watched her recount and demonstrate commands, watched her acclimate them to the borders of the farmstead by walking the length of it in the red afternoon. "These two were always easy," she said. "They're even leash trained. We never had to use collars on them." Sometimes Gil would come, and Anna let herself fall behind them as she had during the lambing. They chatted with the settled radiance of two people who had been together a long time. Something about being away from the sheep farm seemed to brighten them. They put their hands on each other thoughtlessly. An arm, a shoulder. After a while of watching this Anna would realize she was no longer looking at them but at the grass between their bodies, and that she hadn't blinked, and that her vision was blurring slightly, and that the grass was moving in the breeze, and that instead of individual blades she merely saw a numb fuzzy mass of green static. Something loveless, easier to look at. No touch. She smiled hotly. Another success.

But sometimes Gil and Tamara seemed to slow down, speaking quickly and quietly with one another while pointing at the woods between the properties. Anna's interest piqued and she would hurry to catch up with them. But when she arrived the couple grew silent and Anna felt vaguely embarrassed, vaguely abandoned, most of all unsure of how to reconcile the necessity of others with her new way of being in the world.

Even more difficult was the necessity of commerce.

It was a Tuesday morning brushed with light made visible by

mist. She finished loading the viridian stalks of bamboo onto the utility trailer, building blue and gray shadows beside the truck. She set off into town.

As usual Anna was reluctant to make herself known. She sold some of the young pretty shoots of bamboo to a nursery nestled in a row of residential houses, baby plants sticking out of black pots by the road. The old man at the counter asked Anna what other crops were at her farm, but she only said there were all kinds and that she'd really better get back to them.

She sold some of the old dark stalks to a crafts store downtown. From bamboo they whittled candle holders, toy flutes, windchimes, baskets. A bored-looking college student tried to make conversation with Anna but she only smiled, nodded, took her check, excused herself.

She sold the moso shoots to a farm-to-table restaurant by the river. Here the chef sautéed the bamboo with strawberries and sugar snap peas. He asked if she wanted him to fix her a plate, but Anna was already slinking out the back door.

All the money felt like it entered her hands immaterially…She was ambivalent, it wasn't about money, and it was odd to give up such beautiful things for thin white strips of paper, but of course it was about money in the end, after all, that's what this is. That's what it is, as much as I hate parting with the objects of the farm. Money felt like a shadow to the heavenly world of the orchard, two invisible worlds, still very real, in fact violently real, brimming with reality…but they don't mesh, she thought, they don't mesh. My first profit of the orchard. Tamara's wicked gaze flashed in her mind. My first profit of the orchard, money made from the rich repetition of the field…the trigger of the wand in my right hand, the repeated action of the lever in my left. It's not about money, it's about the pure jolts of joy delivered to my limbs. The hacksaw. Sunscreen, sweet sweat and dirt, weeds and herbs. But is there still some pleasure in having a little cash?

She didn't want to feel that pleasure. She didn't like, didn't want that pleasure. It was like the pleasure of companionship. She wanted money to somehow feel irreverent.

And yet—it felt good.

She deposited the checks. In the evening, back home, she sat down at the computer to check her bank account. That's when she saw the email from Jan.

The computer screen was a humming blue box. She read it quickly.

Jan opened by saying how it had been a while, how he'd meant to hit her up now that he was back in town after spending a few months camping, staying with friends, working odd jobs for a few weeks at a time, that kind of thing, the kinds of things she would have loved to do and hear about, but somehow in the time he'd been gone Anna had gone and wandered into dreamland, hadn't she? Rebecca had told him about the orchard. She sends her love, too, says she tried to reach out but had never heard back from you. How's the work? How's the weather? Anna, you're living the life you've always dreamed! I'm so happy for you, I can't wait to hear about it. He continued by saying how he was working on something, a long essay or a short book, not yet sure which, and though it was too complex to explain over email he was sure she'd love it, in fact it might be nice to come and stay at the farm for a while to visit and work on it. He was in the rhythm of travel and not yet ready to get an apartment. He could help out for as many hours as she needed in exchange for a room and some time. Assuming there's a free room? Otherwise he he could figure something out, pitch a tent or sleep on a cot under the stars. Finally he apologized, said he knew it was out of the blue, it'd been so long and he should've reached out before she left. What else? He was smoking again. Cigarettes always seemed to find him in the end. Not to get too theatrical! With love, Jan.

Anna's fingers rested on the keyboard.

She spent a minute or two tracing the square softedged keys, thinking.

Well, she wasn't strong enough yet—she'd only just arrived in her new state—the state of her boundless happiness—her perfect isolation. Jan could mess it up, easy. Him especially. That's what she told herself. That's what she believed.

There could be no disruption. She declined. With a terse, but not unkind, email.

Then she went out to finish the day's work.

One evening she called in the dogs and only Midge returned. Midge wagged her tail slowly. Midge panted happyfaced. Where's Pell? Midge didn't know. Anna called for Pell. The day was blank. No, the day answered: "It's late spring, I don't know anything about a dog. It's late spring. It's late spring." The day which could do nothing but assert itself.

Keeping a still heart Anna went out to look for him.

He wasn't in the apple trees, not from what she could tell, looking down the green and pink corridors. Not underneath his favorite tree or in the shade of one of the sheds. Not watching the ducks with his polite and restrained curiosity, such a sensitive dog. The dogs were good about coming when they were called. She called him again.

When she reached the greenhouse someone answered: "Over here."

It was Gil.

Again he was at the edge of her property. He was standing near the pines crouched by Pell, scratching him along the neck while Pell wiggled around and tried to lick him. There were little tears in Gil's eyes, like dewdrops.

"Anna," he said. He smiled. "I think I lost something here the other day."

"Something else," said Anna.

"A pen, actually," he said. "A pen that means a lot to me. I was just looking for it, that's all."

She was about to say something but decided just to help the man look. They traced the vast green, the grasses and the weeds and the ferns, they walked together, talked a little, found nothing. Anna brooded: the sense of violation she'd felt when she'd seen him there with her dog, the sense of distrust she'd tried to bury…In fact she was certain she'd sensed him at the edge of the property the last few weeks, maybe had even seen his silhouette in the morning darkness. There was some kind of haunted look behind his happy look, like it wasn't just Joe's things Gil wanted to touch but the land itself. That's right, he was relishing looking at all those buildings and objects and trees, unwilling to accept it was foreclosed to him.

"Gil," Anna said quietly. "You can't just come here whenever you feel like it."

"I don't know what you mean," Gil said.

Anna waited. Gil made a groaning sound, a thinking sound.

"I want to help you, Anna," he said. "We've already helped you. We gave you this one, for instance." He gestured down at the dog.

"I'm appreciative," said Anna. "But this place is mine now."

"That's not how I look at it."

"It's the way I do."

It was evening. Purples replaced greens. They were standing right where they'd started, right where the hill melted down into the sheep farm.

She shook his hand before he left. In the morning when she woke to do her labor she checked for shadows at the edge of the woods.

I abjure, I abjure. We reject human company. Don't we? And we live like plants, don't we?

That was what she was thinking at the dogs. It was a few days later. She was walking them through the town, trying to test her new capacities against the world.

She passed the large farmers market by the university clocktower, full of white square tents, softhued produce, the flowerbeds and the retro cobblestone streets, other dogs, children. She'd be there in autumn, she thought blithely.

Where to for now?

There was a time she would've rewarded herself with a nice bottle of wine. Now she was clearheaded. Share a bottle of wine with a friend. Now she was austere. She thought of Jan, who had asked to come to the orchard.

Why keep thinking about Jan? she frowned. He has nothing to do with me.

Maybe a man at the orchard would deter Gil. No: danger is the price I pay for freedom.

She kept walking. She remembered there was a park not far from here. She started heading that way. Hard to keep the dogs under control. They were tugging on their leashes, sniffing around. A pair of students stopped loud and laughing to pet the dogs, interrupting their conversations with each other, happy because it was June, class was over, summer beginning, first real nights of freedom. Anna smiled at them. She kept her distance. The students moved on.

That's how to exist in the world, like the dogs, happy and unaware, unmediated even if you look restless. An almost peripheral existence. Repeat it until it's true.

And are the dogs extensions of me like I'm an extension of the orchard? she thought. Sometimes like sunlight I almost cannot look at the dogs directly. They shine too brightly and say something I don't understand. I can feel something in them I resist comprehending.

She came to a part of the park where the river was slow like thick flowing teal paint. It was zigzagged by bridges. The sidewalk ran parallel to the river, almost mirroring it, carried wrought iron benches like black boats down its length and led up to a gray gazebo. A network of moss grew on the three large stones arranged in a circle beside the water, a sculpture Anna glanced at with the anxious patience of somebody who doesn't understand a doctor's orders.

She entered the gazebo and dropped the dogs' leashes. Nobody was around. And what a strange and pretty night for nobody to be around, with the sun setting like it is. She pressed her hands against the wood railing while the dogs sprawled out happily on the floor, panting and looking around.

She thought again of Tamara, wrung her wrists.

She didn't know how to be anything other than restless. It was hard to communicate the strange things that were happening to her, make herself known in just the right way. To find a way to share in the paradise of nonthought.

She looked out at the pink pale light, sun still setting, she felt in the air the freshness of the river against the dry grass. The dusk was fading from its grenadine light into a twilight purple-blue…a humid, cold, removed color. She tried burying her hands in her jacket. The trees were green or blossoming and one of them was mulberry blackcurrant. The kind of color that stains fingers. Then she removed her hand from her pocket and looked at her own fingers. She felt lately as though she was seeing the world as if emerging from a cold lake, as though for the first time. She felt like she was breathing with the dogs with one lung, with the orchard with the other. She was feeling almost wet from the tremulous serendipity of late spring days. Drinking up the affect of the farm, feeling it intimately in her bones and muscles. Habits make up a life: water, feed, prune, shovel. She stretched, feeling the breeze, free and happy and unaware of how her body might look.

When she closed her eyes it was like she could feel the sound and color of the moon rising.

She felt a sudden certainty that perfection was approaching and no longer asymptotically: she could get there. No matter what she did next, she would arrive. She could get there. She was almost there, able to gaze out at dawns, the light of noons, dusks, stars, almost like she could see them all at once.

But at the same time, she knew it might be true that what she was perceiving as a fundamental rearrangement of the world could really mean that certain sensations were being captured, distilled, purified, plastered over everything. Plastered, and not infused.

Her thoughts were coming slowly. Silence forced its way between each one.

Yes, that overflow would necessarily be tempered, purified, cultivated.

The richness of what existed—it would become almost painfully intelligible.

She wasn't unrealistic.

And then her next thoughts emerged pure and quick and clear. Life was stretching out to its finite maximum, and as she breathed deeply in the gazebo a dog yawned broadly, broadly with the involuntary whine of a dog. And that was that. And she could be tranquil if her perception burned mildly like coals, warm and pink, starry. Like a fact that overwhelms before it's integrated and understood. Right, it wasn't that things would dissipate but that they would synthesize with the part of her that cared for things, brought hay to animals, water to plants, goods to their buyers. Simplicity as her salvation. And what a pretty color in the sky. And the orchard like a garden of seasons, she didn't know it fully yet because she hadn't seen them all, but after experiencing all of them she would overlay them on top of each other, experience all four at once, heat and cold, movement and stillness, light and shadow, color and death. And be complete. After all, autumn will be the spectacular season: when the fruits emerge like birds from a tree. And even with the sad movement forward, such as the death of the plants, the inevitable death of animals, the death of the people around her. And the sky, the sky. She felt herself oscillate dry and wet, thought of moon and tides. She was as light and insignificant as a bird, yes, a bird. Don't look away. Don't be embarrassed. It's all right to feel like a little bird. Here I am building nests in my tall trees, here I am singing a song, plucking worms, arranging pine needles, drinking with my beak from a muddy puddle. See? It's nice. Still, I can make contact with the I that walks on earth. Even still, I can look up from the sometimes-plainness of life and remember the wide warm sky which constantly and imperceptibly changes its shape, pattern, and color. There have always been these quiet murmurations inside of me, like light reflecting rainbow out of creeks, murmurations I've never been able to hear clearly, but have sensed are so vital that to hear them clearly would solve everything. They balk, shiver, and vanish when I strain my ears, like animals trying to cross the freeway. But from now on I'll keep those animals defended with broadshields so that the terror of the world does not destroy them. The interruptive power of a speeding car: it destroys them, obliterates them. Every day I was vanquished. By sloughing off my humanity I emerge as an impersonal knight in silver armor. Life reveals itself slowly like an object painted. The curtain, soft and dark and heavy: it's lifting. And the question of goodness arises multifold, now that I can see where I'm going I can finally think about things like good and evil, things which once embarrassed me to think about and seemed beyond me, seemed less important than the small pleasures I was constantly exploding into my consciousness as though nuance would save me. I who now know the world is divided. So what's the right thing? It really does seem as though the dusk will last forever. And maybe I can even show Jan the wind in the grass, the immense din of stars, owls. Nothing has ruptured me so far, so why not? I can show him how to live divinely. He of all people will like it, and what better thing than to divinely twin this consciousness? (And Jan will return to the city and say: here's how Anna's living. No, this thought didn't occur, she revised quickly, I'd never think a thing like that.) And things will continue to unfold. I'm emerging from something, what? I'm growing stronger. I'm strong enough. I can see uninterrupted and undisturbed—like an eagle. Something is finding resolution. I used to be a sad sort of person, a lonely sort of person who swallowed those superbroad painted strokes very deep within me, because I didn't find myself worthy of them, and if I didn't someone would see me and they would laugh, how embarrassing, I'd freeze like a tadpole beneath a crane, but something is different from how it was before, I don't recognize the little person trembling beneath the swooping shadow of a raptor bird, I don't see the bird at all, instead I glance up and see in the grains of wood and in every pattern I can see the path before me, and see that each movement is part of a long stream of light that will keep flowing, flowing, flowing from the sun even when the sun is gone. Form is light and light is movement. Here's how to describe my movement: I was captured by something which freed me from my abjection. I was woken up from the darkness by chance. It set me on my way. Continuously I flow forward from my first beautiful stride.

She extended her hands in front of her, smiling. Again she touched the wood of the gazebo, which was coarse, rough, dry, full of splinters. She blinked, trying to understand. It would be like climbing a mountain, where every vertical advancement reveals an even steeper slope, and the invisible earth seems to access an impossible curvature. There would be more and more to learn. She exited the gazebo and walked towards the river. The river's frigid movements, cold as she was warm. She looked at the water which was moving. The water was moving. The river like a crystal avalanche, engraving itself into minerals. The river that harbors things that thrive as fast, cold life. It was because she wanted to touch it. She wanted to touch it, lean in, get closer, see it affected, see herself make a mark of gentleness. Join something. The supersymbolic. And she could see her gentle infusion with land, but not with water, and it was only because she was so far away, and the railing was like a barrier, and it was only because from deep within her she felt a sudden craving for her body to be a part of it. Water to water. She who was overflowing with water, thick and warm. Wasn't she? Light and leaves change slowly; water always rushes, announcing itself. It runs almost molten between its banks. Even if it's slow here, swirly. I have to live in every speed. Am I capable of swiftness? Seems I am. See how fast I decided to let Jan in, how I test myself, how I keep myself alive, liquid and afraid. But because she had latched on to something, because she had somehow stabilized herself, instead of hurling her body over the railing, disappearing, and there's the happy end of it all, she spit warmly into her hand, the saliva oozing crassly through her lips, and pushed the warm liquid gently into her palm, and then slowly turned it over, and let it fall slowly, yes, slowly, let it drip down into the river where it was carried off to the ocean to join all the most ancient plants and creatures of the world. The ocean as vast and infinite as the memory of the plains, whose memory? And carrying a part of her own life and by her own choice. Yes, she was a part of things. Wiping her hands on her pants she leaned over the railing, laughing.

7

There he was coming up the hill. Jan. Sitting on the steps beside the bamboo thicket Anna tried to expand her heart laterally the way stillness expands over the disrupted waters of a lake. She was watching. She watched Jan's headlights surge over the little clay hill, heard the jangling of his little red car which was so old and so vivid like a cardinal beetle against the summer leaves. His transition lenses were fully dimmed because the day was so bright, though it was also drizzly, with the raindrops rolling shiny off the leaves and plinking to the ground like piano keys. He was hanging his head out the window. "Hey!" he called. His hair was dark blond and it curled out of his head like gold-plated flowers. He parked his car in a wet patch of grass. "'Sup!"

She remembered Jan as somebody who was always high, who liked to go out at night but was just as happy passing the night with a book in the corner of the living room, curled up in a chair or on the couch, sometimes not even reading but just sitting there smiling as though he had all the time and happiness in the world. He had a way of articulating things where he would stare off into space, dreamy but serious, his eyes immobile glistening and transfixed on some imaginary point, and allow a long silence to pass before slowly spinning his hands in front of his body, as though coaxing the words out from the pit of his stomach, and then finally saying…Jan could say anything, but he'd always put it so blithely, so precisely, so thoughtfully. He was from Sweden. He'd left when he was young, but returned to Stockholm occasionally, and still held on to some fragment of the accent.

She watched him dig around for his bags. She smiled. Jan, tall and gaunt and loud-laughing. He really had done his best to show her what he knew of happiness: how to have a good time dancing, how to be there for a friend, how to live guiltlessly, how to live deliberately, how to be all right putting books down when you feel you've had enough of them. How to not worry so much about money, how to make money stretch, how to pass an empty afternoon without going crazy. How to take yourself seriously as an artist even when faced with the vast nothing, not that it mattered anymore. How to trade off buying things for friends instead of sending money back and forth, it's better that way. How to live!

So how could she have declined? She was indebted to him.

All this was surging up in Anna with the violence of a flash flood: Jan's absolute and total image.

And now Jan was coming up into the wet world. Today it was a cool bright blue, and it was morning, and the apple trees in the lightly watered field were soaking up that blueness through their roots and mixing them into their green leaves, and above Jan's red car the clouds were rotating slowly in the sky as if he himself had summoned them. Meanwhile Anna was still trying to open up her heart. She posed with a tranquility she did not fully feel on the steps of the cabin. She tried to make her anxious smile look serene. Her hands folded. Dogs at her side. Her heart pounding but still she tried to look as though she were welcoming Jan into the gates of heaven. She tried to embody that phenomenon which had erupted into her psyche with the onset of summer and bloodcrystallized by the river. Jan would cure her lingering sense of loneliness—in a sense Jan would replace everybody else in the world—and in return she would find a way to impart that phenomenon to him. She knew it was a risk. First he would have to let go of something, like a plant that wordlessly relocates its nutrients when the top half of its body is severed. Then things would appear for him like when fog rises thickly and reveals the bottomless depths of a valley. She didn't know what to do, she tensed, feeling the light pang of intrusion she didn't know what else to do. She tried to welcome Jan with open arms, even though when they hugged his body was so surprising sweet and unfamiliar that she couldn't remember even seconds later what their first words to each other had been. They were at the kitchen table.

"So, the reclusive painter, alone in the woods!" Jan was in the middle of saying. "I thought it couldn't possibly be as beautiful as the photographs. I always knew you'd sequester off into some cabin when you were older, but here you are already."

He was right. She felt like a struck clock bell. Vibrating, furious, happy.

"Here I am already," she repeated.

"Thanks for having me."

"Of course," she said. "It's good to see you. Sorry I hesitated."

He had been leaning over the wood with his bony shoulders, and to show his forgiveness he closed his eyes, sat back up, smiled sarcastically, and exaggeratedly shrugged.

"When I said I would help around the farm I meant it. The last thing I want to be is a burden for you."

"You don't have to help."

"Really?"

"Really, I'm just happy you're here."

Jan seemed to consider the offer. He glanced to the side.

"But I want to," he said. "I like that sort of thing."

Then, still smiling, he looked at her too frankly. She broke his gaze. After all, she doubted having him in the orchard right away would work, it'd have to be slow, otherwise he would disrupt something, interfere psychically somehow...if only she could lock him up in the attic, she thought, let him affect things gradually, an hour or two at a time...

Instead she explained the work and her schedule. He promised to make breakfast every morning, except if he slept in: and she couldn't fault him if he did. She laughed. She asked after his life. How long had it been, two years?

"Where to start?" he said. "After my mother died I quit my job and moved in with my friend Andrew, who was living in Asheville. You remember what she was like. I could finally just do what I wanted. I brought my laptop, my notebooks, and about forty bucks. I was grieving, but I mostly felt absolutely liberated, like I could finally do whatever I wanted without judgment. No one to answer to. No one asking where I am, what I'm up to, why. Which made me feel guilty." He paused. "Guilty and free. I bet you felt the same."

Like a deity his voice filled the whole cabin, and when he stopped talking it was like everything was waiting for him.

"I didn't know your mother died," she said. "I'm sorry."

He waved it away. "I didn't announce it," he said.

Silence. He was still waiting for an answer.

Joe struggled to materialize. Dark shadow trying to form on the wood of the wall.

"I guess I did feel similarly," she said.

Jan smiled and resumed his flow of speech. "After three months Andrew was sick of me. Some misunderstanding over a woman not worth getting into. I had been writing remotely for a nature magazine, but I quit when he kicked me out. I was ready to change everything. I spent a few months in Canada, working temp jobs under the table...After that I bought a tent and a hotplate and camped through Tennessee, Oklahoma, Texas, Arizona. Probably saw enough stars to last my whole life. I stayed with my friend Valerie, you don't know her, whose family owns a garlic farm in California. It was nothing like this, of course. So dry and drab. Jesus, look at me ramble." He laughed. "What can I say, the only thing I'm good for anymore is finding places to live for free."

"Camping in a dark field," she murmured. "Sounds wonderful."

"I know that kind of thing is harder for women. You can't just pitch a tent and forget about it. But look at you, your life isn't so different. We're not."

Jan had maintained eye contact. Anna took her time responding. She cracked her knuckles and smiled, slow and unassured.

"So I'm your latest couchsurf, that's all?"

He smiled back.

"That's right, that's all."

They laughed again. It was hard not to like Jan, so magnetic, the way he ended his sentences as though anointing them, the way he could defuse any tension. Maybe things would be fine. She went to the fridge and got them some oranges. Sitting there in the kitchen, dyed by the light from the bamboo and the rainclouds and the stormy sun, Jan looked like a tourist in the morning tropics, digging into his orange with a short clear fingernail. He was out of place everywhere, but confident in his leisurely way of handling things. A luminous, innocent confidence, like a hero's.

"Beautiful trees, beautiful flowers… I didn't tell you in my email because I wanted to see your face," he said without looking up, "but the piece I'm writing is kind of on Charles Burchfield. That's why I knew I needed to come up. You remember him?"

"Of course."

Her work had often been compared to his, both by Jan and by what few critics had paid her any mind. Not that Jan had any formal relationship to art: just his love of things touched by the dreamworld, and enough conviction in his intelligence to write about things he had no experience in. That sense of the eternal beginner: that blend of naïveté and curiosity. For Anna, Burchfield had her same interest in the psychedelic aura of nature seen close up, extreme light, extreme color, a stained-glass perception, flight-into instead of flight-from.

"Burchfield is the organizing principle, anyway. I want the piece to sprawl, talk about all kinds of lives, philosophies, moments in history. When you read a perfect piece of nonfiction, the flow of logic seems obscured but feels perfectly organic, don't you think? Right now I'm trying to talk about some of his early paintings, which look to me like Japanese woodblocks, with the same fluid black outlines. From there I want to find a way to pivot to a section on Siegfried Haase, a criminally underrated German painter, expat to Canada."

Suddenly Jan cut off. He was wringing his wrists and looking down at the wood of the table.

"Maybe that's silly," he said. "You're the painter. I don't have the vocabulary."

"It's not silly," she said automatically.

He nodded, happy to be reassured. He was like a child in that way. She told him she'd be happy to take a look at the essay. "Maybe a book," he said. Maybe a book.

Anna studied him while he looked for one of the early paintings on his phone. Jan embodied some kind of new color, didn't he? Strange against the shadows of the kitchen. He's a little more anxious than I remembered him: or maybe I can see it better now. But one month in the country and he'll see his own hue reflected somewhere.

He showed her the painting. *Clouds over a House Top*.

"Yes, you're right about the Japanese influence," she said.

"What about you?" He took back his phone. "Is your studio in one of the sheds? I'd love to see it."

"No," she said. "I haven't been painting."

"Not even a little? On the floor or something?"

She stood up, restless, and got them both some water from the tap. The green bamboo light had faded, it was raining harder outside, and the roof wasn't tin but drummed nicely anyway.

"No?"

"Not really," she said. "I just lost interest."

She set his water down. He tilted his head but seemed to decide not to push it. He took a long sip; his gaze floated all around as he searched for another topic. His eyes were blue and clear.

"Tell me what it was like when you left. You just left? And left Patrick, just like that?"

How could she explain that he'd meant almost nothing to her? She couldn't stand the idea of sharing a life with someone, the constant incomprehensions.

"I just left. I don't know why I stayed for so long."

"He didn't really understand your work, right?"

"He liked my work."

"Sure, but he didn't understand it." He traced a ring around the rim of his glass. "Not to drag it out, Anna. I just always thought your paintings were so brilliant. I think you stayed with him so long out of comfort. You've always loved comfort."

"Maybe."

"But not practicality, and Patrick was precisely the opposite, at least as I remember him. Moody and practical, and such a pessimist."

She smiled. "Right, you never liked him," she said.

"Even if I had, and it may seem cruel to some, I would have understood you wanting out. You were together so long and never seemed happy." He adjusted his glasses. "You have to find your own autonomy, right?"

You do, she thought. Jan isn't so different from me. Neither of us likes to be constrained. Though Jan's way of being in the world was more of a blithe embrace of freedom, compared to the abstract pain she felt when life bore down upon her. Jan loves to feel liberated, I love life-without-suffering. Jan loves the void and I fear it. For him the void is joy. She was looking down at the table. Seeing a thousand different grasses, seeing a thousand permutations of the same field…at the same time she felt jealous of how easily life came to him. He said something.

"What?"

"I said, now you seem happy."

And the way he was looking at her indicated he had some idea of this new aspect in her, her primordial revision. That's the attitude of someone who can be saved, she thought.

"I am," she said gently.

She closed her eyes, refocused her beams of light, looked at Jan anew. Don't be jealous of your friend. Share with him. Mix together. She stood up, felt herself radiating.

"Do you want to rest?" she said with aggressive gentleness.

"I'd be happy to." He stood up too. "A warm place to sleep is like a cocoon, Anna. Don't you think?"

"Like a cocoon?"

"Like the warm cocoon of a caterpillar."

They climbed the ladder to the second bedroom. She'd already prepared it for him. The spare mattresses were stacked up in the corner; his was in the window by the sunlight, dressed with fresh flat linen, one austere pillow, an orange-and-blue wool blanket. A new wood desk and a plastic chair. "It's adorable," Jan said. "My own little garret!" He took the afternoon to unpack. Anna went out to do her work.

She arranged the apple maggot traps so she could hang them in the morning and she gathered in a big canvas bag all the unripe windfall. Now she was free to feel all her fear that Jan would distort her image of things. She closed her eyes and tried to imagine the orchard in all its discrete parts. She was worried the earth on to which she had grafted her perception would flatten differently under new feet, and Jan would walk around in the grass as though stepping on her face. Already the new and immense muteness of the orchard. But through a gigantic concentration on the new budding apples she might be able to maintain things despite the new presence. And the orchard would swallow them as a body accepts an organ. Difficultly, completely. It would tie them to the knotted roots of the apple trees. Somehow their disparate identities would dissolve and be reduced to the same substance, the substance of the farm, and the two of them would find a way to occupy the land together.

Their first day passed with rapid grace. In the late afternoon Jan spoke of his intention to use what money he had to buy a grill and some charcoal, nice new lanterns for the porch, a bistro table for breakfast and books and coffee in the mornings, a hammock for books and tea in the afternoons…He'd build a firepit using the raw stones of the earth so he could pass his mornings like this: sitting outside in the cool blue air before dawn, reading by the porch light, his library books stacked up beside him with their milky solid colors as though incompletely conjured in a dream…He'd put the book down, go to the kitchen, slice bread, toast it, retrieve eggs from the ducks, break four into the skillet, and make breakfast for the two of them in the morning flame, the smoke mingling with the mist and the dew, the fire a flash of pure red light in that pale dim groggy world. Then they would eat together in the emergent sunshine.

And after breakfast she imagined him piling his books on the bistro table and then there would be Jan, tall and thin and bending over the book on his knees, his glasses almost falling off his nose, his pen held between his slightly crooked teeth. Unthinking or thinking hard. He'd wave at Anna when he saw her working. Sometimes help for an hour or two. Then go to his room to write until dark. Then turn on his lamp and write some more. And his black silhouette would linger in the high yellow window, presiding over the night like its overseer.

Yes, they each thought. That's how things will be.

That evening they took a trip to the beach. It was an hour away. They saw the black cliffs and the sea so light and silver. Jan mentioned how certain he was the work would go well, how electrified he was already feeling at the orchard, and asked how Anna didn't find it inspiring for her own work, you know, the paintings, yes, she felt him needling her again, and at that final gesture at the old life, his words proffered before the woods and the winds and the ocean breeze a little too cold and even stinging their faces, Anna balked and replied: Jan, even better than making something is living something. Wouldn't you rather live in one of those paintings than observe one, see psychically the waving colors of the field, extrapolate rainbows from a single point onto an entire field of vision, see the spirit of the woods in the woods?...He didn't reply. You'll see, she thought. You will. Things grew quiet. They went to a restaurant to eat oysters. They ate at a table by the window. As Anna broke open the sickly yellow shell to eat the animal inside, feeling furtive, feeling decadent, she peered over at her friend and tried to silently communicate something of her thoughts to him. But Jan was busy constructing the perfect bite: he didn't want to taste the raw, slimy muscle of the animal. He wanted to taste the cracker with its docking holes, the animal which was a living mass of flesh on top, the red spicy sludge of the cocktail sauce, he was completely immersed in the sensory pleasure of eating. A tiny squeeze of lemon. He opened his mouth wide, looked her in the eyes. Ate it. Loud crunch.

Outside the restaurant, through the big windows, a white streetlight ignited and smudged against the glass. When they stepped outside, Anna blinked slowly in the electrolight...there was a rainbow sphere clinging to the tip of a brown eyelash. She blinked again and it was gone.

8

Just a few days later Jan managed to break something. The toilet. She was shattered awake by his shouting in the middle of the night. Her heart was still beating as if recovering from a nightmare as he cracked open her bedroom door. His guilty face appeared in the gap.

"Nothing here really works right anyway," she said. "It's all right."

"I know. It's kind of charming," he whispered from across the room.

In the morning she drove to the hardware store to buy a new wax ring. She spent the afternoon fixing it. She felt Jan watching her work through the door to the living room. He was lounging on the dirt and grass-smelling couch with his books pages pens notebooks scattered over on the coffee table. Thinking what? The day passed. Shadows formed and heat swam around the cabin with nowhere to go. He didn't say a word to her.

But at night they took a walk. The road was thick with trees whose leaves blocked out the sky. It felt to Anna like they were walking through pure blackness, almost purely abstract space.

"You're so handy now," Jan was saying. "I'm impressed. When we met you were so helpless, like a bird in a flock, always awaiting orders."

She was shining a strong flashlight out before them so the world was that void and within it a circle of light. She couldn't see his face.

"You would've been so overwhelmed if I'd broken something, in fact the whole world overwhelmed you, you used to cry so easily, practically anytime something happened to you…medical bills, fall-outs with your friends, like with that woman Yancy. You were so sweet and naïve. Now there's a calm in you, I've noticed, a stillness. Maybe this place has changed you, or death has sobered you, or you're just a serious property owner now."

She felt like he was smiling but she still could not see. Her limbs felt numb and she frowned invisibly. The scent of pine was overwhelming. Jan sometimes liked to test her. She tried to angle the flashlight to catch something of his face, but caught nothing, just more ground.

"I don't want you to think I've given up or failed or something," she said.

Jan said nothing. They walked on for a minute in silence before she spoke up again.

"I never cared about a career. Painting was something I did in pursuit of a certain way of living. You always used to push me to work harder…I never wanted that, it was never who I was. I wanted to understand and process the world without language, to see it through shape and light and color. Like when I look at the trees in the orchard, for example, and see them less as trees than as solid-somethings interrupting air…it's about how to look at things. And I find that in simply living here more than I ever did in art."

Her heart was constricting like a wrung rag. How many times would she have to explain it? Jan was silent for a long time. Were they suddenly enemies? Meanwhile up ahead the black trees were parting: a world of dusty dark blue light was making itself visible.

"That's brilliant, Anna, you ought to write it down," Jan said quietly.

They arrived at a neighbor's horse ranch. Whose? Anna had never seen it before, she had never walked so far this way. The grasses of the pasture were dyed blue and purple by the night. Far away in the center of the field there was a woman. She was reaching out her hand to touch the neck of a horse, the only horse, it seemed, unstabled at this hour. They were having some kind of slow secret intimacy in the night. Jan and Anna walked up to the edge of the fence.

"Here with all your dreams from childhood, memories from the time we're loved and cherished and protected, and everything is fantastical. No, I don't blame you."

Jan watched the woman with the horse with attention and tenderness, as if thinking: so here's the real secret stuff of this life: its intimacies. Meanwhile Anna suffered. So Jan knows nothing of the inhuman anonymity with which I'm living. How deliberately I'm annihilating.

Not like this, she thought, surprised at her unhappiness.

9

It was almost July. It was time to work, and Anna readied herself for the transference from the pastoral to the georgic she had foreseen in the gazebo. But before she could bring Jan into the orchard it was imperative to confirm the psychic nature of the place still existed, so in the middle of the night after she was sure he was asleep she rose from her bed, went past the dogs sleeping on the yellow porch, past the bamboo grove and the summer garden, past the halfbuilt pond near the duck run and out into the apple field above which the stars were reflected in the night sky, as though a star had formed within each apple bud and floated up to burn. Yes. Night remained the time for thinking. That's what the orchard was saying to her, and squinting she felt as though she could draw vaportendrils of the pink scents of fruit up into the lights of each star. She walked slowly in the darkness, running her hands along the shadowy branches, inhabiting things. That was what she saw. How long since she'd really gotten here? She emptied herself. She paused with one bare foot above the grass…she completed the step. Dozen of blades parted on her sole. Her apple garden. The light-dark of hot nights. The mirroring.

Then she stood still in the apple grove, absentmindedly rubbing a leaf between her thumb and her forefinger. It had rained and the leaf was wet…She imagined if it had kept raining, overflowing. The ducks swimming in the wet soil, the wet soil coagulating into mud, the apples mutating into mangroves, the farm lightly submerged, the farm becoming a floodplain good for rice and cranberries with the rain coming down abruptly as though heaventossed in giant handfuls. And the water eating everything, mixing with the trees and the grasses, mixing with her body and Jan's and everything else's. That's what she hoped things would be like…and even if the way things were going to be between her and Jan was still forming (and she loved that word, "things," so malleable), even if they were still figuring exactly what things would look like between them, how their friendship would revive and transmute itself, after a submergence like that the two of them would have no choice but to sink into the grass, attach their feet to the root systems, and share in the nutrients of all those apple trees. Together, the thousands of them.

Then he'd understand.

Jan's window lit up. She froze as though it were a floodlight. She saw his black silhouette in the yellow window. She squinted, but couldn't tell if he was looking out at the summer darkness or opening up his laptop to work.

She returned to the cabin and went to sleep.

At first they hardly spoke. They had no need. Each had their work. Jan took over a few independent tasks to ease himself into the rhythm of the farm. He made them breakfast in the morning, wrote and read throughout the day, and cared for the animals, the rabbits, ducks, cats, and dogs. He seemed primed to forge a special bond with the dogs. (And they had done excellently, like sentinels: Anna hadn't seen the bear in months.)

Coming back from the orchard for lunch one day she saw him reading aloud to them as they lounged on the cabin steps. A passage from Thoreau or Emerson or some other transcendentalist, one hand holding the book by its spine, the other plunged into Midge's thick fur, rubbing her neck absentmindedly while his cigarette burned in the plastic ashtray…by the time he finished his sentence Jan was shaking with emotion or anxiety. His voice quivered and so did the book. Then he set it down, took a long drag, and exhaled. He seemed pensive. When he saw he'd accidentally blown smoke into Midge's face, her large eyes stinging, he leapt to his feet and waved away the cloud.

He rubbed her head. "Hey, hey," he said. "There it is."

It was a new gentleness. But what was affecting him? She felt unable to access his inner life. Would he have read that passage to me, she wondered, or just to my dog?

When she began to take him out into the orchard, she figured she would start him off easy. After breakfast one morning they went out to prune. Since the springtime the diamond-pink blossoms of the trees had fallen and dusted the dry ground like tinted snow, and now the fetal apples were thinking of burgeoning, the red spheres slowly revealing themselves from within their green cocoons, blending oddly with them, like green skin grafted onto red sclera…In the daylight Anna could see them in all their horror. No veil of soft night. The lower branches were stiff and the apples were unfolding in clusters while the flower buds curled up hard as rocks, petalless. And on the ground the unripe windfall looked like an evisceration.

Together they trimmed the younger aphid-laden branches so that the fruit-bearing spurs could access the light. Anna reached up with her gigantic red pruner on top of her ladder, watching the limbs fall to the ground. Then the sun settled on a branch like an incubator while the apples formed like eggs. And with their thick green coats of leaves each apple tree looked so colossal, so much taller than a person and with so many lives (worms squirrels butterflies ants aphids bees birds spiders) within it that to work at its side was like examining an enormous breathing animal. And there were hundreds of them: hundreds of red-and-green animals, rhinos, elephants, standing perfectly still in rows on the slope with its carpet of bushes, ferns, and flowers.

But was it the same for Jan?

For long stretches of time they were silent together, and Anna couldn't think of anything besides whether or not Jan was experiencing the same divine contact, and couldn't feel anything but the frustration of having her own contact blocked by his presence. Because although she tried to close her eyes and sink into the apple trees as she had done so often, even as they were growing unfamiliar to her, to access that feeling-beyond-the-verbal, to purely feel what the trunks would feel, to understand the birds' warbling in their own language…her thoughts were blocked like a river by a rock. And how to get around it? She snipped off a watersprout. Even standing on the ladder across from him, separated by the body of an apple tree, it was like he could see into her thoughts. And yet could not understand them. They couldn't formulate properly. They died. Jan would see the doleful look in her eyes and ask with ironic, playful affection what it was Anna was dreaming about.

Which knocked her right out of it. It isn't just dreaming. Besides, Jan, you mean to say you're not dreaming? Then what's on your mind?

Outside the orchard things were different.

He was attentive. One night she was sitting in front of the computer staring redeyed at numbers and prices, trying to comprehend them. She was picking at her skin and nails when Jan's large hand appeared out of the corner of her eye. He had brought her a big, cream-colored mug.

Grassy, savory smell. Stinging nettles. His pale wrists were pink with irritation.

"The gloves didn't help," he said.

She was touched.

"I try to wear long sleeves and at least two pairs."

He invited her to join him for a break at his bistro table. They sipped their tea quietly in the warm night. Because Anna was cultivating emptiness, she directed the conversation toward Jan, and they began to talk about his writing. He complained that he had always preferred simply presenting readers with passages and felt less interested in analyzing them, and thus degrading them, than in allowing the juxtapositions to speak for themselves. But he couldn't write it all like that. He said he wished more criticism had room for abstraction, artfulness, nuance.

He went inside to get his copy of Burchfield's journals. It was a massive book which took up the entire bistro table when Jan set it down and opened it to a bookmarked page. She read where he pointed, his finger framed by the yellow light of the electric lantern and the dead moths around it:

> Within the earth's shadow, which was a deep luminous slate blue, already the night sky, appeared the first "stars"—a bright planet first and then "Spica"—long before any stars became visible in the rest of the sky— The dead grass in the foreground lit up by the western glow.

Jan said the entry was written in 1946, the same year Burchfield finished *The Sphinx and the Milky Way*, though he had started it nearly three decades earlier. They looked at the painting on his phone, and then at the same painting in another of Jan's books where the reproduction was larger and more insistent on its beauty. The stars and the garden, thought Anna. Jan kept talking about the painting's place in the essay, the dilatation of time, the triumphs and despairs that true art demands, but numbly Anna was thinking, gazing out in the direction of the apple trees, which she knew were looking back at her. The stars and their garden.

Jan went on. He said Burchfield moved to the country young, like you. He was always in crisis, like you. He was a painter, of course, like you. Like me? she thought. That's how Jan thinks of me. There was something in this conversation she found embarrassingly precious, and it was more than just her desire to get on with her life. She remembered the softness of the brush, like eyelashes or a child's stuffed animal. The apparent primacy of color over meaning. She knew she wasn't being fair.

Burchfield wrote: "Life for them performs itself—They do not know what it means to contemplate suicide—Love is as simple as eating to them." True, that's what Anna felt, too. Life came so naturally for Jan. He didn't have to fight for his happiness.

Burchfield worked steadily in the woods, died uneventfully of a heart attack at an old age.

And me?

And why this impulse to narrativize? Jan shut the book. He was smirking to himself.

They went to sleep. "I would have loved to see him paint more animals," he continued over coffee in the morning. The morning sun was dusting the kitchen table and the back door was open to the breeze. "Blue deer like Woody Crumbo's, but more smudged, more impressionistic. At least in his late period. In his early one, I think the animals would have looked monstrous, like in a Germán Venegas painting. In that evil-looking painting of a church in a storm, for instance." Again he showed her the paintings on his phone.

He had said it with the slightly condescending look of a friend nudging you toward some future trajectory. So that's how it is, she thought. He sees me not as a person who has made a choice but as someone to be saved.

"I'm sure his animals would have been lovely," she said noncommittally.

"You should paint a little portrait of the dogs."

She broke his gaze. It was too much.

"Let's get the pruners," she said.

Sometimes the reverse would happen. Mild, happy, sociable, the two of them would have an easy streak together in the orchard. They smiled. Their muscles slackened in the blurry sunlight. Trying to pass the time, she'd say something to Jan:

"This tree's budding nicely, isn't it?"

And Jan would simply hum back at her.

She peeked at him through the branches of the tree, noticed the worried expression on his face, and realized Jan was probably thinking about his writing, was that it? So distracted. Why couldn't he talk about it in the orchard as easily as he could outside of it? His face on the other side of the row was half-obscured by the brown trunk with its black veins and random branches, like a natural prison framing his face. He was at work hacking off an infected-looking limb. And as if peering into the wooden cage, Anna stared and tried to decipher his expression. Hopefully, if he wasn't able to talk about his work, and wasn't able to talk at all, he was experiencing—something. She wanted him to admit it.

Then she lowered her eyes, feeling foolish. Finally, setting her hands to work again, hanging her pruning saw on a particularly stiff branch and pretending to observe the angle of her cut, she asked with feigned casualness:

"What's on your mind?"

Jan looked at Anna, surprised, and each time with some slight variation said:

"Oh, it's nothing." Setting his ladder against a new tree.

"Nothing much." Holding onto a strong branch to steady himself.

"Not much." Pausing on the ground, his hand on the railings.

"Nothing at all."

And then he would smile.

Afterward, as if finally understanding why Anna had initiated conversation, Jan tried to talk to her about his writing, people they knew, cooking, the news, anything. These conversations did not satisfy her either. She was waiting for him to detach himself from his awareness, see raw images, be swallowed by them, admit to being swallowed by them. The apples are a wondrous thing. Why was everyone so intent on deciphering the world? Sorting color into form, form into technique, and water into objects instead of letting them all leach waterily into one another, like salt and soil.

She wanted him to lift the film separating one thing from another. Sometimes he said things that made him seem so close. The painting of the world they lived in: wet, half-painted, paint in the process of drying, paint in the middle of its imperceptible chemical changes, paint outpouring into air.

The wet season was arriving. It was going to rain for days. Sometimes Jan spent his afternoons doing something or other in town, he wasn't so detached from the world, he still needed it, so while he was out Anna lay in the orchard where it was drizzling lightly, she was looking up, she was wide-eyed and grass-stained and luminous…he came home while she was sloughing clumps of mud off her clothes in the bathroom. She heard him up to something in the kitchen. She looked in the mirror, wiped dirt off her face, then went into her bedroom to change into dry clothes. And when she came out there was Jan: lounging on the couch with two glasses and a bottle of vodka.

"I picked up a really nice one," he said, "so you have to sit and drink with me."

He had already filled both glasses with ice. He motioned to the seat on the couch beside him. She sat down.

"I was reading Tove Jansson's letters the other day," he said. "You know, she did the Moomin books. Have you seen the cartoon? You'd like it. It's cute. Anyway, what do you think of this?"

He leaned close to her. He read from his phone in one hand while the other, holding his vodka, rested near her shoulder.

"'Every artist portrays not only themselves but also their time. Do we know the face of ours, yet, though? My canvases are praised, admittedly, but in a rather cold and respectful tone—while there's lively criticism of my 'restraint and lack of emotion'…maybe I paint too much with my brain (though my heart is in despair over every picture).'"

Jan clicked his phone screen off.

"Well?" he asked.

"What?"

"Don't you agree?"

She didn't answer. Jan's face was flushed. His look was intense, unfocused. She tried to move away from him but she was pressed against the arm of the couch.

"I'm sorry," he said. "I get nervous."

"Nervous?"

"In situations like these."

He was looking at her with frustration. It was dark. It was still. The leaves were green. Something inside her ached sweetly. Then it collapsed with geometric violence, the way a building collapses.

She coldly looked out the window at the orchard.

Jan backed off.

"You say the Ruby Beauties make a nice cider?" he said.

"That's right."

"Hard cider, right?"

"No. Well, maybe. I don't know the process."

"It can't be too difficult. It's just fermentation."

Jan played with the ice in his glass, swirling it around by rotating his wrist.

"Never mind. Let's make a hard cider anyway. It can't be too difficult," he said quietly.

"Maybe." What had happened?

"You can learn a process. Let's look it up now." He started typing on his phone, then stopped. "You could still sell it, couldn't you? I bet it would be profitable. Do you need some kind of license?"

Anna blinked. When she took a sip she frowned.

"I wasn't thinking about that. I thought we would drink it."

"Selling's what matters. After all, you have to make money, don't you?" He downed his drink, then smiled at her. "Dreaming, dreaming," he teased. But his voice was harsh.

He poured himself a little more vodka.

"I looked it up the other day. You can make beer with the honey locust pods, too. That way you don't have to choose. We could build a whole brewery on the property." He reached over to top her off. She could hear the frustration in his voice. "You could, I mean. You could do anything if you're really going to spend the rest of your life here. What a life, Anna. A quiet, abstinent little life for Anna. Anyway, it doesn't look like you need a license."

He set his phone down. She stared at her drink. All she wanted was for him to say: red, green, red, green, here I am snipping the little branch crawling with chartreuse bugs like the fur of a green cartoon monster, trail off looking at it, who cares if we're behind schedule with the pruning. That's peace. Instead of humming, thinking, drinking, snipping away indiscriminately.

She looked at Jan, his downcast eyes. She felt a sick feeling of betrayal.

Betraying what? The window. Something.

'That's a good idea," she conceded. "The beer." The glass was so cold it hurt her fingers.

In the orchard they had moved to the Teratourgima rows, those gigantically mutant apples, which even in their embryonic state were bulging and growing so rapidly they looked like fresh wet tumors. She was getting better at fighting Jan's delustering effect. She was occasionally able to access that feeling-beyond-the-verbal, but it would always break right apart...For example, she would sometimes look up and see that the sunshine was reflecting above her on the leaves of the trees that were so high she had to look at them purely vertically and almost dizzily she would notice that the leaves seemed to shimmer like a flock of pure white birds...But then, in an instant, it was just the dull gloss of leaves.

Again she tried looking, this time down the long line of trees dizzy again as they curved up and down the hill and gazed back at her like a hall of mirrors. Right, because she was one of them.

Then they were just trees on a hill.

Finally exhausted, she looked at Jan, who was settled in his thoughts. There he was.

She needed to construct a space of solitude. Somewhere to think, somewhere to observe the orchard from a different angle, and not just when Jan was away or sleeping. Where? In the fields he could watch her from the attic window. From the packing shed you couldn't see a thing. She settled on the greenhouse: it was doubly separated from his vision and, from the hill where it stood, overlooked some of the trees. She slipped in one afternoon, sat down in a plastic chair.

Every day those green buds reddened and expanded. And because it was her first time growing things she identified the feeling with the light pang of creation with which she was more familiar, the materialization of the something-tangible you could anticipate and almost dread. And she had the feeling that if things went wrong, if the apples were underripe or sour or mealy or rotten, it would be a personal failure, not a failure of circumstance or taste or even really of technique—a purely personal failure. Apples don't deceive you. It's simple. You grow something edible or you don't.

Something stirred. She looked. A cat was in the greenhouse.

That light pang of creation. She was feeling a secret desire, something shameful, running parallel to and against the work of the farm. All this talk of Burchfield, Crumbo, colors, artists, outlines and nature...doing it again might be wonderful, a net of oils, God prowling around the fields, auras and sweet surreality, it might even help her see things the way she was seeing them before Jan showed up. That's right, she thought, I can still do great things. Why not me?

But perhaps my feeling this at all is Jan's dark influence.

That's right, I was perfectly happy not feeling these things. These are illusory desires.

Then through the glass she saw Jan emerging from the cabin.

Jan who hadn't bent to the will of the orchard as she had hoped. She was scared. As though Jan would destroy that special perception before she found a way to concretize it in the world, to prove to other people it existed…and it really existed, she thought a bit childishly, it did…

Jan looked left and right and all around and then he spotted her in the greenhouse window.

He spent a long time wading through the tall grass. He took exaggeratedly high steps, like a gaited horse.

It's not fair, she pleaded with herself, I don't want to feel this way, I don't.

Jan arrived. He opened the sunshine-yellow door and just stood there.

The light came in broad and strong from the enormous patchwork windows of the greenhouse, and a square of light sewed itself onto Jan's cheek, whitening his already pale face. It was a clear blue day.

"This one looks ready," he said, fingering the leaf of a tomato plant. The fruit was half green, half red. He picked it from its stem and set it by the door. Then he took a seat in another one of the plastic chairs, putting his head in his palm and looking at Anna. "Tomorrow I'll make us…pan con tomate."

He said it with a flourish. She smiled. It was hot and quiet in the greenhouse.

"How's your work?" she asked.

"It's all right. I'm stuck, completely spinning my wheels. I feel like it'll never get off the ground. But I actually don't feel like talking much about the specifics today," he said. "I'd rather just think about what a nice lunch we'll have together tomorrow."

"That's good," said Anna. "We'll take a nice long rest. Rest is important."

Resting wasn't what she really meant, of course. She was looking at him with heightened attention. He had lifted his head from his palm and was leaning forward in his chair, hands clasped. He smiled ironically.

"What do you know about rest?" he said.

It was hot and still in the greenhouse. She didn't move. Jan leaned back in his chair, backing off a little, stretching his legs out in the dirt in front of him.

"I'm resting right now," she managed finally, a bit nauseous.

"You're just sitting there."

"I like sitting here."

"You were always a little hermitic, Anna, but never like this. I'm worried about you. You have to live life. Let's drive into town tonight, find a bar."

"Instead I think you should put down the writing for a while, take a moment just to be here. Then sitting for a few hours wouldn't seem so strange to you."

"I can't put it down. It's the whole reason I'm here."

Dimly she realized she had grabbed on to a container pot as though to balance herself. She was softly touching the black plastic. And gripping it with increasing force.

"Take a day to walk through the woods," she tried again. "Don't speak or write or even think. It'll help."

For a moment he seemed convinced. He was silent for a long time.

But then he said: "No, no." A bit agitated. "You're missing my point. None of this is relevant. How long are you planning on staying here?"

"Here?"

"At the orchard."

She was surprised. "I don't know, indefinitely." She thought a moment more. "I live here."

"For the rest of your life?" His face had started glowing red. "All your talk of looking scares me. You can't just look at life. You have to live it. You have to make something of yourself."

"What's wrong with how I'm living? We can't all be nomads."

"You looked almost sick when I got here. Anna, you can't just wall off forever then die."

But what's really better than dying all alone? Anna thought. Nobody to mold you, nobody asking you to pretend you're something you're not before death. A little loneliness is a small price to pay for absolute stillness, absolute peace. Here I'm not anything at all, she thought, not even a woman, thank God. Jan of all people should understand that.

"Jan, bring your chair over," she said suddenly.

Jan picked up his chair and set it beside her. She asked him to turn his chair to face the windows. He hesitated, then obliged. Their hearts were beating. She was going to show him. She wasn't going to talk about it, she couldn't find the right words, but she was going to show him anyway. With words, Jan had the upper hand. Everything was starting to make sense. In order to force Jan into the nonverbal she would have to use nonverbal means. Look out at the grass and plants, waterlogged and so full of movement and color despite the stillness, a movement and color and world of life beneath the grasses. She took his hand, large and pale and soft. Softer than hers, roughened by work. Because without a hand to hold Jan might lose himself. Jan who still needed language. His hands were clammy. Metals are blocked from glinting by the opacity of the soil, she was thinking at him, earthworms are squirming and rubbing up against the minerals, lots of little minerals like the ones in our bodies. You can just see things. Like the tree trunks, like I was saying: not as a something-solid but as the absence of flowing air. We'll join in like inosculated trees: branch to branch. Limb to limb. Even our green leaves are touching. Here in the greenhouse where the seeds are germinating.

She had been holding his hand loose and warm. She tightened it. I'm leading you as though leading you through the underworld. It's like we're visiting Persephone. The bar? We're going to the bar with Persephone. You can feel the borders of the orchard extend upward and downward without clear limits, from the underground rivers to the fires of heaven...see the barely shimmering surface. She tried to twist his hand a little, to force him to go there. Sometimes pain shows us the way. See it! "It's a life of pure instinct," she thought, or did she accidentally say that out loud? Jan seemed to flinch when she thought it. Maybe she said it. She willed herself not to feel embarrassed. Everything's a little imperfect, after all, even when I'm showing Jan the way. He started breathing differently. Softer. Her grip relaxed. She felt embarrassed. She tried to tighten it again. She had half a mind to throw him to the ground, shove his face into the earth, smash his glasses, force him into comprehension the way she had forced herself. Maybe he just needed to feel the dirt on his face.

But Jan's instinct said: I'm bored.

He squeezed her hand the almost sorry way one squeezes the hand of the terminally ill.

So she had been defeated. She lowered her eyes. What could she say?

"In the orchard, I don't think as much," she mumbled. "I feel at peace. That's all."

Jan was still holding her hand. He rubbed her knuckles.

"I think I'm different from you," he said.

She shook his hand away.

"Anyway, no one can forget themselves all the time," he said quietly. He stood up, seemed to be consider his next words. His face looked fallen.

"But you used to seem so full of life, especially after a day you spent painting. Now you seem—" He paused. "Well, I don't know," he said.

He remained for several more seconds, seemed to decide not to continue, and went out.

She was holding on to the black pot again. She listened to the greenhouse door close. Maybe Jan will leave the greenhouse and the afternoon will paralyze him. Listening to his footsteps in the grass she was trying to believe the afternoon was paralyzing him. He was growing lost like a child. He was about to pause and be altered. He had understood. He was stepping out to understand. Surely. She had shown him.

Leaning limply over the eggplants, overcome with sudden revulsion, she almost vomited.

They passed a few days hardly speaking. Jan expressed his care through the dinners he made. Ratatouille, pan con tomate, gazpacho with cucumbers fresh as waterlilies. Lamb kebabs. They piled up dishes and she didn't wash them. Jan did. She got ready for bed.

They finished pruning. There's a new distance between us, she felt, as though both of us are embarrassed by our forcefulness. August arrived. Late summer, flies, cicadas. Dark green, an invisible sense of gold. The final task of the season was to install new drip irrigation. They began to uncoil long black polyethelene tubes in lines parallel to the trees.

Spending so many days outside together in the sun, and for such a long time, they would sometimes get dizzy from the expanding heat…and then the air would grow heavy with humidity, the colors of the world would saturate, and kaleidoscopic fractured rain would fall upon the fruit. Then they'd put on their boots and raincoats and work through the wetness. But the heat lingered. The mood of the orchard seemed to conjoin itself to Jan's mood, which might have meant that Anna's mood conjoined itself to Jan's. He was either happy with how his work was going, lifting his face up to feel the water, leafing breezily through his books and papers at mealtime, or else he was stiff and frustrated, depressed about his inability to excise the essay of whatever he felt was bloating it, or convince readers some quasi-transcendental painter was worth caring about. Nothing is, he'd say spitefully. He'd apologize to Anna for getting in her way and lock himself up in his room to stare miserably at his laptop screen. Then she would be left alone. In those quiet days she felt softly toward Jan, guilty for her impatience, even as she kept doubling back to correct his careless placement of the irrigation tubes looking like black snakes in the grass.

The whole world was sweating. She was alone among the trees. She could hardly keep a schedule and at times worked past nightfall. It was becoming clear they would need to hire help for the harvest, when she knew the work would be even longer.

Abruptly the diamond largeness of the orchard faced her as a stranger. Like it was laughing. Did you think you could do it alone? But there must be a way. But then I have to keep Jan around for the harvest: because I won't have to pay him.

What did Joe do? She didn't know. Gil rarely came around to talk anymore. She had always imagined Joe, during those flashes of weakness in which she allowed herself to imagine him at all, solitary, struck by peace, his low voice swallowed up by the fields and the winds, ruminant, solitary, thoughtful, happy. Happy despite the solitude? Or because of it?

Then, on a day Jan opted to work, they came across a cluster of damaged trees. It was at the eastern edge of the orchard. The trees seemed to have been pushed over and raked as if by claws. The berry bushes had been trampled into jam. Part of the wood fence was broken.

"What's this?" said Jan.

Anna stared dumbly at the trees. She crouched.

So the bear had continued like a gleaner. Unless the damage was old? The tree seemed a bit rotten, corrupted. Greenish wisps of life were emerging from the bark like floral maggots.

"From the storm, you think?" said Jan.

Dovelike innocence.

It was a hot, cloudy afternoon. She felt miserable, violated, desecrated. The orchard glowed a dull yellow. The sun was shining on the wreckage as if from farther away than usual. Even the daffodils in the grass were melting.

"It's the bear," she said flatly. She stood up.

"The bear?"

"A black bear that comes and eats the fruit."

"A black bear," said Jan, weighing it.

The green grass swayed. She looked down the row of trees in the direction of the cabin. Though she could not see them, she knew the dogs must be watching. They would be staring silently in her direction, their faces smudged by distance, expressionless and incomprehensible.

"The bear's why I have the dogs…"

Slowly she looked over at the trampled fence.

All she could do was look, look around like an animal.

Like Jan the bear had dragged the orchard back into time.

Then it seemed to click for him.

"The dogs have to fight?" Jan cried. "You make those little dogs fight?"

And as though to atone for the dark secret of their existence Jan made it his mission to show the dogs that they were loved. The afternoon grew foggier, sunnier, and through the veiled strong sun and soap bubbles he gave them a cold summer bath. He filled up big shining metal vats with water, hosed them down, and rubbed soap like seafoam into their fur. Pell yawned sleepy and happy, Midge splashed around and snapped at the bubbles. All three of them disappearing in the light…Jan treated the dogs like they were friends.

Watching them from the stoop she realized that she did not. Before Jan arrived, maybe. Now they were tools. She went inside, tried to busy herself with the dishes, but felt compelled to resume watching them from the window. The dogs had grown to love Jan too. She had the impression meanwhile of having condensed herself into a cold dead stone. She realized she had never heaped such boughs of love onto anything. Not even when the dogs had defended her, not even when they ran up to her like proud children.

She had a new, fleeting thought, something thinkable only because in that moment all the other organisms were preoccupied, so she could be daring, so she could consider something with bravery and with distance. It was a small thought, expressed obliquely: something about the impersonality of great rainbows when compared with the smaller rainbows glimpsed in opals, or in the running waters of a garden hose.

10

The next day, late in the afternoon, Gil and Tamara came by to look at the damaged trees.

Jan had not yet met them, nor had Anna told him much. He observed the couple with quiet interest while Anna walked everyone to the assaulted corner of the orchard.

She had been thinking: for the trees to have lain so long slaughtered and unnoticed—since, after all, they had grown tiny green tendrils of life—she must have been too distracted. Her apprehension dimmed. And it wasn't just the enormity of the summer fieldgrowth, since there had been plenty of times before Jan when her brain and body had seemed able to stretch out and conquer the whole thing, even if that only happened in flashes or fragments like tectonic plates. She tried to listen but heard nothing. Or instead heard: boots on the grass, incomprehensible birds, Gil's inane and nervous observations. So something had been severed.

Something had been severed and it was probably Jan's fault.

Meanwhile the light of the day was gilding the plants and the evening was stretching and warping the dark shadows of everybody moving. Gil, Jan, Anna, Tamara, the dogs, the apple trees, others. It was dry. It smelled dry.

"Thankfully it's only a few trees," said Gil, looking down at the wreckage. "You could always just let her munch a little! Her cubs are probably hungry teens by now."

Jan laughed. So here's your company, he seemed to be thinking when his eye caught Anna's. He seemed to like Gil. He leaned gingerly against the part of the fence that wasn't broken, looked at Gil and said: "If they're anything like I was, they won't be able to help themselves."

The two men glittered at each other.

Gil appeared to like Jan too, or at least seemed reluctant to meet Anna's eye.

Then there was Tamara. Silent, stoic, frowning, reigning over things. She stood there thinking. She had the solid and inflexible quality of an immense object.

Only Tamara was looking appropriately severe, as if searching for someone to discipline. Only Tamara was looking appropriately analytical with her jewelcut face unmoved by humor.

Six bodies spangled and dispersed around the ruins of the trees, like the nearly symmetrical petals of a holy flower.

It was quiet. No one spoke. Everyone waited for Tamara.

Tamara took Anna aside. Jan and Gil immediately began to joke about romance, imagining for the bear an absent suitor, her abandonment, her womanly rage. They played with Midge and Pell, tugging their ears and messing up their fur. The dogs were growing, distancing themselves. They were taking on the demure statures of porcelain bulls.

"Come by this weekend and we'll talk about what to do about this," Tamara said. "Bring the dogs."

11

Their front door was open. But the bug screen was closed and from behind it every few seconds came a hard slicing sound. The day was overcast and cool. Anna approached.

Through the screen she could see Gil working on something at the plastic table. The netting diced her vision of his face. Today he looked rigid, pensive: he whose unhappy looks had always seemed so fleeting…He was carving whole fat frozen hens into quarters and tossing them into a plastic crate beside him, beak feet gizzard and all, ice crystals rigidifying their feathers. He was making giant cubes of dead chicken, their severed sides revealing congealed and frozen blood and organs, incomprehensible like an abstract painting…When the crate was full, he set the meat saw down and took the crate out the back door to where they kept the deep freezers.

Returning he saw Anna in the doorway.

"Anna," he said. He fingered the plastic of the crate in his hand, seemed briefly happier. "Go around back. Tamara's in the pen with the red gate."

She nodded, thanked him, and left, aware of him watching her as she went out into the fields and the pastures unfolded and she found the red gate. Gil had made her anxious, why? She looked ahead. Here the grass was long and studded with clover. The sheep in the pasture: freshly shorn like smooth wet marble. Tamara's image materialized gradually: Anna could just barely make out the body of a ewe in Tamara's rough hands, Tamara moving the sheep around with a palm under its chin and the other near its tail, Tamara's long black hair draped over her curved back like a goddess, she was probably shearing off wool like foaming water, as though birthing the true body of the animal…

But as she neared Anna saw that this sheep, too, was already shorn. The sunny pinkwhite of its body glowing. Instead Tamara was sticking some kind of blue gun up into the corner of its mouth. She glanced at Anna and returned to her work. The ewe's nose was caked in blood and mucous. Her nostrils seemed to be writhing. She stomped around. She bleated. When Tamara finished the ewe swallowed uncomfortably and stumbled off into the dirt.

"Where are the dogs?" Tamara asked.

"Out front with some of yours."

The ewe was no longer a revelation: just an animal in pain. Newness had popped like a bubble, deflated and banal.

"We'll take a walk. I'll drive. The trail's not far."

At the trailhead Tamara bent down to check the dogs' teeth, holding their heads with the same unforgiving grip she had used with the ewe.

"They're looking good," she said. "I thought their teeth might be hurting. Sometimes when they don't do their job it's because they're in pain."

They entered the woods. Tamara had brought some of her dogs, too. Not too far into the walk the trail approached a lake shining despite the cloudscape like a vast chunk of lapis. The mud on the trail was greenish, pink underneath, and the moss and lichen on the rocks around them left an electric trail of blue.

"They're eating enough?"

"Yes, just like you showed me."

"Not overheating?"

"I don't think so. There's plenty of shade. Their water's in the shade."

"Have they killed anything?"

"Not that I've seen."

Tamara thought on her own for a while and then sighed.

"Some dogs just don't take to the work."

Anna felt her heart pound. "Maybe there's no bear," she almost whispered.

"I thought so too, but Gil insists. He says it's just like when one came around a few years ago. And he's spent much more time over there than I have. I don't know anything about trees."

Anna considered. She knew she had sensed it, known its shadows. The dogs had known. Yes, it was out there.

"Have you thought about an electric fence?"

The orchard electrified…

"No," Anna said.

"It would help with deer, too. Not too expensive. Do you have a rifle?"

"No."

"We'll go and get one. Expect to spend a few hundred. Who's the man staying with you?"

"Jan."

His name lingered in the air like a question. Tamara glanced at her.

"Does he have a rifle?"

"No!"

"Everybody needs a rifle."

Another silence, like the dark weight of a gun.

"Don't let Gil convince you otherwise," she added.

It had started drizzling and she could see the rain falling into the lake with a thousand rapid blooms and falterings. Moving green muck and algae, maybe? Pretty and organic. The trail hugged the edge of the lake then ascended. Slowly it began to shrink from her vision. Anna had a sense of being thrust forward into time: she realized it was autumning early here, a few brown leaves.

"You want a gun no matter what," Tamara continued. "We never used to have one. Then we had a terrier get ripped apart by a coyote. Gil had to beat it off her with a shovel. But it was too late. After that, I insisted."

The rain churned. The dogs wandered around the women like fish.

"They were so tangled up with each other that a shot might have killed both of them. It still would have been better."

A rifle, Anna thought. She turned it over in her head as if with her hands.

"So he's an old friend?" Tamara asked. "Not some freeloader, I hope."

"No, he works."

"Good. You can't afford to have someone just hanging around."

"Well," Anna said. "He's going through a hard time."

Tamara frowned. Their conversation fizzled out again. They were speaking haltingly the same way the rain was stopping and starting above them. Away from the orchard she felt the world looked softer. Nice to walk with someone in the light of day instead of hiding in night's nonmemory.

"He's not just an old friend, he's a dear friend," she tried to go on.

Who was she trying to convince? Tamara glanced at Anna and again did not respond. She let the topic go. They paused to look at the ruins of an old lime kiln, ivy in its belly. They paused to look at trees that looked like demons. According to Tamara, there used to be houses around here, but they had all been demolished to construct the reservoir.

Not a lake, Anna understood, a reservoir. That's why the water was so purely blue.

They arrived at a clearing. Two perfect logs, dry beneath trees, an ashed-out wet bonfire.

"Let's take a rest," said Tamara.

She sighed as they sat down. For the first time Anna saw the heaviness in her body, the bags under her eyes, the tightened jaw.

"The slaughterhouse?" Anna guessed.

"The slaughterhouse?"

"You seem tired."

Tamara's eyebrows lifted as though she were surprised to see herself watched like that. She started ripping dry wood off the log like a little girl.

"The slaughterhouse doesn't affect me like that, it's just a pain," she said. "I'm surprised Gil hasn't told you—then again, maybe it makes sense that he hasn't. Our neighbor is trying to expand and wants to buy some of our pastures. Gil and I can't come to an agreement."

Tamara rolled up her sleeves, revealing clean undirtied skin, muscle.

"I want to sell," she said. "It would be less land to maintain. I could cut back hours at the slaughterhouse, and we could reinvest the money into our equipment. We could pay off debt. Gil doesn't want to give up room for the sheep, but we have empty paddocks all the time. They'd have less space, sure: still plenty. To him the idea is intolerable."

Her voice was stiffening.

"The reality of the situation doesn't matter to Gil. All that matters to him is that things look nice and peaceful around him when he wakes up in the morning."

Anna was going to comment but Tamara went on like heating iron.

"And I'm not as cold as you might think. I want our animals to be cared for. Gil's response to all this, for some unthinkable reason, has been to order twenty more head. No market in mind, just a breed he likes, like dolls. It's the absolute last thing we should be doing. It's something a toddler would do. It's the kind of thing Joe would have pushed him into."

She cut herself off. She positioned her body away from Anna.

"I didn't much care for him," she said. A harsh smile. "I take it you didn't either."

Anna couldn't think of what to say. She was just watching Tamara. She was so close up she could see the silver in those black hairs, how her face and dirtied clothing almost reflected the hue of the landscape, like it had stained her.

The silence went on and on and then became so brittle Tamara had to shatter it.

"But it's not like I hated him," she said. "He tried to be a good friend to us. We moved here after he'd already been here a decade, back when the sheep farm was just an overgrown plot of land, the house practically uninhabitable. We were terrified. Two young people dreaming of country life, peace and stability, just like you. Gil's parents owned a grocery store so he knew something of this world, whereas my great-grandmother had owned a few animals, that's all. I never met her, but I always felt so kindred to her as I saw her in photos, looking simple and sunbaked and happy with an armful of chickens. I felt more connected to her than I did to the family I actually knew.

"Joe showed up on our doorstep same as Gil did you—in fact, I think you represent of a kind of debt for him. Joe helped us get running water in the house, build out the porch, the living room, sheds, shelters. He helped us transport and vaccinate our first twenty head. We had almost no neighbors then. The woods around us were almost as thick as yours. But there was more of a sense of community, Gil's right about that, so we settled in well enough. There were flea markets, fairs for more than just tourists and corporate sponsors, we were good friends with a U-Pick berry and flower farm, a vegetable farm whose name I forget, run by two sisters...we all used to trade with one another. I never had to buy chicken from the grocery store.

"Joe taught Gil about regenerative agriculture, herbalism, biodynamics…he spoke a lot like you, so emotional. He used to talk about how he wasn't strong enough for the world, how he had to reduce it to what he could control: his orchard. I wouldn't understand what the hell he was talking about until I got older, not because I felt it myself, but because I saw it develop in Gil. The two of them would sit together by the fence for hours, talking about nothing, watching me while I sweat and bled in the heat. He convinced Gil to stop banding the lambs' tails one year. But who has to brush the shit and piss out of them every day? Not them. Three ewes got fly-strikes that year. Some of their flesh was completely liquified. They were full of awful ideas. I caught roundworm from a sheep because Gil didn't quarantine her long enough. He said she looked lonely."

She rolled her eyes, as though loneliness were a ridiculous concern to have for an animal.

"Things like that. I know I make them sound like idiots. A lot of things did work I said wouldn't. Like the clover. And it was his idea to get a lot of dogs, because he knew I loved them and had always wanted them, and that we could use them supplement our income. The dogs are my life. I like the sheep, but I don't love them like Gil does."

Tamara paused, as though guilty, then went on more quietly.

"The only ewe I ever really loved was a Rahmani ewe, small and reddish, the only one in our flock. I bought just one because it was just the kind my great-grandmother had kept before immigrating. The other ewes rejected her, of course…Actually, she's buried on your property, in the woods between our farm and yours. There's an easement there so we can visit, something Joe got on paper officially." She paused. "Which was kind of him."

Tamara stopped talking.

She spent a few seconds alone, suffering from the wound of time.

"We don't visit," she said. "I don't, anyway. And Gil told me you asked him to stop coming by. He's—well, he's been torn up over just about everything since Joe died. Someone had to knock some sense into him."

She looked away. Whatever expression had appeared on her face was hidden and then obliterated: when she glanced back over at Anna, she had returned to her natural stoicism.

The fact was that Anna could not fully comprehend death and its aftershocks.

"I'm sorry," Anna said.

"Why? He was your kin. It's your loss, not mine."

What to say? He was nothingness. Was there pain in that void? Tamara looked briefly angry. Then, again: nothingness.

They sat together for a few minutes. The dell was alive with plant and animal life. Suddenly she could hear it all: birds, frogs, bugs, snakes, nutrients running, chemical signals.

"I'm going to pee," Tamara said eventually. "Excuse me." She disappeared into the trees.

Things sublimate.

With Tamara gone, and the diluted green light in the trees above, and the shadows beneath them cleaving vision itself in half, she took a moment to breathe with the animals.

The world felt as though it had faded to black. As though things had shifted. The singularity of two moments divided by a long, slow, black blink.

Who do I have? she thought. Jan and the dogs. Jan understood her renewing impulse, at least in part. From how Tamara described him, Joe might have too, had they known each other during his life. She held Tamara's story in her mind. Joe appeared as a dim figure equal and opposite to her, warm, blurry, someone who was better suited to photographs than reality.

She called Midge up, looked into those dog eyes. Why my reluctance to love you too? You're already so much closer to Jan…it struck her with the instant dizzying harmony of an enormous gong: how much the dogs had been trying to love her.

She understood it instantly but also slowly, complexly, and with difficulty, as though removing a fiber from a brittle crystal fleece. She uncoiled a hard sapphire thread from that iridescent tangle of wool, thinking:

There's strength in persisting despite someone's incorrect perception of you. The only kind of interpersonal perception there really is. Refracted, distorted by relations. I don't know any of these people, any of the animals, not in the way I'd like to know things, a totalizing knowledge. There are only these tangent points…Midge and Pell always touching my knee with their noses. Trying to reach me sensitively, trembling with pride and begging for approval.

She scratched the dogs behind their ears.

Tamara reappeared and hiked on.

The new silence between them had none of its former stiffness. Both women were digesting and Tamara's limbs now swung easy and loose.

No one else had to know these things. In fact everyone could probably sense them differently.

Anna looked at Tamara. Coldly Tamara smiled under Anna's eyes.

Meanwhile the clouds were beginning to disappear as though purified. Sunlight bubbled down into the wet forest. Pooling on the forest floor like expanding dollops of paint was the light, expanding invisibly as the sun progressed. The forest was ripening in the evening and the white bark of the trees looked like diamond stakes. Anna thought the hyaline film of water over roots was like the water of birth…The rainbow scales of beetles refracting as if divinely stroked. And down below, the reservoir had contracted with their increasing distance, from something immense to the size of a little blue jewel, as if the moon itself had sunk down into the pit of the forest and shrunk, leaving behind the lush blue crater that was the body of water.

At the top of the trail the trees opened up and revealed to Anna her first aerial view of the world she now lived in. The colors of the autumning leaves looked like thousands of painted spades, almost glass…and the papery rainbow of the leaves opened out onto the rocks of the crags, and beyond the rocks of the crag was the belly of the forest, and beyond the belly of the forest the town, the fields, the almost rootlike connections of the roads.

She and Tamara stood on a sphere of rock just big enough for the two of them. Tamara took a seat on a dry patch of stone, stretching her limbs out in the sunshine.

"Here's the view," she said, brushing away leaves and twigs. Her voice was flat.

Mountains looming in the distance. The town spread vast beneath: no clear borders.

Her first thought was: so all along I have been dissolving into things impossible to observe from the ground. Things that encompass and extend beyond the orchard, which for me has been everything. Here it was.

So she was a separate being from her orchard, which she had tried so hard to graft herself onto. Like a dog in the fields, or a duck in its run, her limbs would never petrify and rise like the trees from the indifferent soil of the earth.

But she could graze, hunt, forage, fertilize…and with her own bone marrow.

She blinked in the new brightness.

From far away things looked less magical. Things looked like they could be dominated. She didn't like that feeling. How horrible to see it all at once, every rank and file of the world! Thankfully the orchard itself was out of sight.

How horrible to see the thick wall of plant life continue like a weak membrane before revealing abandoned factories, trucks overflowing with goods moving in and out of town along those rootlike roads…restaurant chains, new and old cars…the world in its disgusting movements.

That's right, she thought, I don't want to grasp the limits of life. Somehow it's being forced on me. The town ends there and becomes the interstate and clings awfully to everything.

Where's the compromise? Slowly she looked across the town, looking for something to love.

She tried to imagine a well from which she could pool up happiness. She was unable.

Maybe it's better to say the orchard has invaded me, somehow. And I still retain something of that essence.

Suddenly Anna felt sad, exhausted. She didn't know how to feel, what to think. She felt alone and like everything had become very difficult.

To not be alone she turned to Tamara and said: "I think you should sell."

"That's surprising to hear you say," said Tamara with her cruel lilt. "Of course, I think so too."

Don't people tell each other what they want to hear in order to be comforted? But Tamara didn't seem all that comforted. She was scowling out at the landscape just like Anna.

12

Was a more modest happiness possible? Long nights, food and friendship, connection, nature, conversation? It felt like a step backward. She was willing to try. She could alter or at least quiet herself while still retaining the secret thing within her. After their walk she went gun shopping with Tamara, felt the weight of weapons in her hands, felt the much more tangible power of something heavy and absolute and with the same wood elegance as an apple branch. The men who sold it looked amused. But she went home with a lightened spirit and a calmer heart: the heart of a woman with a gun.

When she got home she set it on a cabinet in the living room, submerging it in shade and height and dust. The dust smelled nice, grassy. She went back out to water plants before nightfall.

In the morning she saw the gun had disappeared.

Of course it had been him. Who else? She spent some time contemplating the fresh emptiness. Then she climbed the ladder up to his room, gingerly so as to not sound angry, lifted the trapdoor, and poked her head up to look at Jan.

He was lying in his bed with pillows scrunched up against the wall like a makeshift headboard. His body was buried beneath the wool blanket, and his face was lit by the blue light of the laptop living on his stomach. Books and papers littered the floor, as usual, some dirty clothes, a water bottle, pens. There were two mugs by the lamp on the bedside table. Midge lay in bed with him, already so massive she weighed down a corner of the mattress. It wasn't easy to help a dog off that ladder…and beyond the mess the big glass window, the morning light, trees the sun pressed color into as though destroying them by fire.

She saw that he was crying silently.

The rifle was on his desk, radiating in the light.

She climbed up the ladder and sat down in the space between him and Midge. She pet the dog.

"What's going on?"

He shook his face red from crying and kept looking at the screen. He tried to reach for the mug with coffee in it but his hands were big and clumsy and he knocked over the lamp and it shattered.

"Fuck." He scrambled to sit up in bed. "I'm sorry."

"It's okay, we'll buy another one," she said. "Are you all right?"

Jan's face plunged back into despair. "Are you?"

So that's all? she thought. Then there's no worry. And the same way I treat the apples I want to treat to my friend now, right?

Unfamiliarly, as though doing something inhuman, she reached out her hand to stroke Jan's shoulder. Her other hand was still on the dog. As though a chain of love could link the three of us. Jan flinched at her touch and looked at her alarmed.

"You don't have to worry about me," said Anna. "I'm not striving toward some future thing. I'm happy."

"You've given up. You're not well."

"No, I haven't. This is my life."

Poor Jan…she smiled at him. He froze for a moment then smiled too, but that smile was followed by another tremor of tears.

"You're writing in bed now? Does that work?"
"I haven't written anything I've wanted to keep in days."
"Then let's clear off your desk," she said. She got up. She picked the glass shards up off the ground and put them in Jan's trash can. A shame, it had been pretty, red green and blue.

Then she got the rifle and took it downstairs.

That's right, she was willing to try. They could attain a new harmony.

She tried to imbue in Jan the same time and attention she gave the orchard. I offer myself, she thought. I go through human motions. They drank. They slept late and waited until the afternoon to do their work, drinking coffee in the heat for hours before spraying the trees and combing through the orchard underbrush with their scythes.

She was used to cleansing her own feelings for the benefit of someone else, as she felt she had done in the last life, and at times she really did believe that she could do it, could share some kind of real human happiness without depleting her psychic reserves: such as when Jan collapsed drunk and happy in the orchard and almost fell asleep with his head by the roots and grass and embryonic apples, or when they revisited the night farm which by day was full of horses, brown and blonde and spotted, or when they hung hammocks up and slept outside with the dogs, or when they finally finished the duck pond and watched the flock swim between the stones. It was the closest Jan had come to experiencing the abstract thing—she saw him forget himself, saw time paralyze him—and for a while she thought things might work out.

They drank some more. They drank in the house. They drank outside. It was always balmy. Fireflies, night spiders, mothwings, moon. When Jan was drunk he fell all over Anna, collapsing in her lap or talking in her ear. Night after night, he had a lot to say:

"It's true I haven't written as much as I'd have liked, but my mind does feel clearer, slower...I think I might visit my brother in the winter…I think we should go into town more, meet some other young people…My friend Jard works at an urban farm in Denver, I wonder if he'd like it here, you'd love him…There was a horrible sex scandal at the gallery I worked for, I can't remember if I told you…What, are you going to marry some farmer?…Can't be many young men around here…Let's make kimchi…Your friends are a little odd, aren't they? The woman's a bit of a bitch, and the man is kind of a clown…It doesn't matter, I like them anyway…"

Sometimes Gil came to walk his flock through the windfall. He was quiet, serious, alone. Then Tamara came to see the dogs. They never came together anymore, but there was an uneasy silence in them both, as though each could sense the recent presence of their strained love.

Another night on the porch, the full moon, the summer garden glowing with color despite the darkness. Jan said something about liking being at the farm. How he was beginning to feel rooted here, how surprised he was he liked the feeling after so much wandering.
"So I'm the friend you've stayed with longest?"
"You are. I usually only stay a few weeks at a time. What's it been, two months?"
"Just about."
"What can I say? It's all too much for one person." He gestured out at the orchard, toward all the prepubescent fruit standing obediently in the darkness. "You need me."
They laughed together. They were laughing more often and with new ease.
"I will need to hire another person or two," Anna said. "We won't be able to pick them all alone."
Jan considered. He had set his drink on the top step. Now he

picked it up and rotated it slowly between his palms. Anna was frowning, a bit anxious now. Why? She drank.

"Don't worry," she said. "I have the money for it."

Jan glanced up at Anna then downed the rest of his drink.

"I mean it wasn't that much," she explained. "Enough to get started."

"No, I wasn't thinking about that."

He made a joke about someone they had both known. Anna laughed longer than Jan. She was thinking about the money.

He made dinners.

"You've become quite the cook," she observed. Caprese salad, salmon stew. He always set the table ornately. A candle glowing on the wood table, common flowers in water.

"You're just noticing?"

"You used to be awful."

He laughed. "That's right, I could barely make a pot of rice. I ate out all the time. What can I say? I ran out of money and had to learn to care for myself."

He twirled his fork around in his salad. "It's relaxing… When I'm cooking it's like that's all there is."

They ate lavishly. Some days they didn't work at all.

She decided not to install electric fencing: she didn't want Jan to stumble into it drunk. She decided not to apply any insecticide stronger than neem oil: the pests stuck to her sticky traps and didn't seem to meet the threshold. She decided to keep Jan around, even at the cost of her own melancholia. He was needed.

Another morning in the greenhouse. She was thinking. She was fulfilling Joe's dream of the permaculture orchard, fulfilling it even though she hardly knew him, had her own reasons for doing what she was doing, and was superimposing her own on top of his. There was something mysterious and gratifying in fulfilling the dream of an absent person, wasn't there? Another person's dream: how strange. A stranger's dream. To live a life that was not her own: psychedelically suspended above the world as though viewing it from another plane.

And she had nearly convinced herself things didn't need to be perfect. That she didn't need to asymptotically approach perfection. That she could love the growing apples even with their faults, those strange crescent bruises and flecks of dirt, here and there the wilted leaves. They're not identical: it's a whole tapestry of information. What information? I don't know. But how did I ever find them so perfect?

And whenever the strange divine feeling threatened to touch her, she sought ought Jan out and spoke to him. The plain warm sun. Life could be easy.

The fruits were growing larger. They ripened.

Unobserved, they were breathing in the orchard like a sea of silent mouths.

13

They went to a diner not far from the highway. Across from it were wind turbines, a big dry graveyard, a gas station. It wasn't busy. Faced with Jan across the booth, Anna continued practicing her humanity.

A draft of Jan's manuscript was on the table, and he kept his coffee near it as though eager to spill something on it. The brown liquid and the red pen.

"Anna," said Jan. He pushed over his book. "What do you think of these?"

He opened one of his books to some industrial scenes from Burchfield's middle period. Smoke, warehouses, factories, roads. None of those psychedelic paintings of foliage.

"They don't speak to me as much."

"Me neither." Jan sighed.

"Then why bother with them?"

"You don't get a full picture of the guy without them." He reached over and turned the page, showing Anna another gray-and-black painting. "Looking at these makes his landscapes seem so empty in comparison. But when people do appear, they seem depressed, almost ghostly. Happiness is emptiness for Burchfield, humanity and industry malaise. That's what I've got to touch on."

The waiter came by with some coffee. Anna didn't look up. She just accepted it, then drank: strong and nutty.

"More sadness in these, more reality…" Jan said. "And back to the sublime at the end of his career."

She flipped through the book. *Burchfield frequently castigated himself for his human desires, which he feared made him unworthy.*

She glanced at Jan. He was watching her closely. As she looked at him he gulped some coffee down.

She beat away the feeling before it arrived.

"Can I talk about something?" she asked.

Jan nodded. He pushed away the stack of papers to indicate he'd give their conversation his full attention.

"There are a lot of possibilities for the future, aren't there? It only took a few days for you to build the duck pond. I could try to permaculturize the apple fields, take as much labor out of the equation as possible. I could plant new trees. We could refurbish your room as a whole dormitory with those extra mattresses, invite more people up, make a community of it… I've been afraid to do much of anything with the orchard, but it could be something different, something special. Couldn't it?"

Jan was smiling but his eyes were narrowed. His glasses looked foggy.

"It's a great idea," he said quietly.

She nodded.

"It'll be nice."

"It will. We'll drink to it!"

They clinked their mugs together. Anna looked down, didn't smile. It had not felt good to say. Maybe it isn't possible to force yourself to want something you don't want. But at least she had made Jan happy for a moment.

It was quiet for a while, quieter than when they had arrived. Lunchtime was ending. Theirs was the only table left. She checked the time on her phone. How does a place so big and empty turn a profit, she wondered, looking around at all the empty tables.

Then she wondered again, astonished at her own thinking: Since when have I thought of things in terms of profit?

Their server came by to refill their coffee. Anna looked up at her for the first time. Boughs of braided black hair, heavy dark mascara. She looked about fifty.

"Can I have some eggs, please?" said Jan. "Two, over easy."

"Of course."

She walked away.

"If the eggs are half as good as the coffee, I'll be happy," Jan said. He rubbed his temples. "I'm so hungover. What's the name of this place again? Thompson's House?"

"I don't know."

"Thompson's or Thomas's. There's something about it on the placard outside. Historically a place for farmhands and mill workers. It makes sense if you look around."

The server came back and gave Jan his eggs. He cut them open with his butterknife.

"I don't like to read those things," Anna said. "Places are what they are. Why think about how they got that way? We should just experience them."

Jan made an ambivalent noise. Eventually the waitress brought the check. It sat there on the table until Anna picked it up to pay.

14

She had no idea how to advertise, hire, employ, or negotiate wages, but somehow she was able to find two men through an advertisement she placed in the local online newspaper. *The Bullion.* The flat artifact-dotted image of the farm appeared in a cramped square beneath articles about a new school principal, a policeman who'd saved an animal from traffic, a massive power outage…she offered twenty-two dollars a bin. She'd wanted to offer less. She'd run imaginary numbers. Jan had disapproved. She'd stared at the harsh bright liquid space of the computer screen, waiting for responses.

Sean's email rambled: he was a student, he'd wanted to work on a farm abroad last summer but it hadn't worked out financially, it seemed like a good thing to do while young, he was uncertain about what he wanted to do in life, he needed some time to think, why not take a semester off to pick apples in his hometown, he wasn't in any rush to graduate, he was ecstatic to have stumbled across her advertisement, what luck, no need for board, he could live with his parents and commute, he didn't even really care about the money…Victor's was simpler. He was an experienced farmhand. He offered no context. He asked about lodging. Jan told Anna he would be fine to split the attic.

They picked Victor up from a bus stop. The sun was low as they drove home. He was a talkative man with a paradoxical air of solitude. Halfgray hair and features made small by melted wrinkles. He asked to test the wood apple ladders.

"These are okay," he said, shaking one back and forth in the darkness of the shed. "Not the sturdiest, but they're okay. When I was heavier, I broke a rotten step beneath me. But these are okay."

For dinner Jan made a cheese and meat spread with butter, toast, lightly braised vegetables. Something easy. Anna fetched a bottle of wine they were chilling in the root cellar, and when she returned Victor was telling him a story.

"Someone I knew tried a moneymaking scheme in Indiana," he was saying. "On a tomato farm. On the big farms, the crops have to look perfect. If they aren't perfect, we have to toss them. After picking, the farmer had us drive a truck full of imperfect tomatoes out into the woods to dump them. He didn't care where. He just didn't want them rotting in the fields. My friend had the idea to take those imperfect tomatoes and sell them to the Mexican grocery store in the city, where he was already a regular. They didn't care whether or not a tomato was ugly. For a while he and his friend with a truck made almost as much delivering imperfect tomatoes as they did in a day of picking, but when the foreman found out, of course, they were fired. Idiots."

Jan smiled and said, "But it worked for a time, didn't it?"

Victor just shook his head.

"When Anna and I lived together, I tried everything in my power to avoid having a job…I must have tried dozens of moneymaking schemes. I wrote horrible fictions and passed them off as things that had really happened to me, and I tried to pitch them to big magazines, magazines with payout. No luck. I played the lottery, I thought about importing Swedish snacks and overcharging for them…I might have been a little drunk for that one. I've always been chronically broke. That's one way to live." He glanced at Anna. "Well, it's not like I'm ever late on rent, am I?"

They laughed while Anna poured the glasses. Jan asked Victor about his family.

"No, no more. My parents died, I lost contact with my siblings. I've been here about twenty-five years. When I came at nineteen I came with my uncle, who died a few years ago." He rapped his fingers on the table. "When I was a teenager I played in a rock band. Las Pantallas. We broke up when I went off with my uncle. Want to see a photo of us?"

"Sure."

He took out his phone. His phone was old and caked with dirt. There were four boys in the photo, standing in a line and smiling near a restaurant patio.

"That's you with the shaggy hair?" Jan asked.

"That's me. We played at that bar every Wednesday."

Anna looked. His guitar was electric blue and bifurcated by a crack on the phone screen. The leader of the band had a white guitar and the others held drumsticks and a bass. The drummer's sticks were raised above his head in an X.

Victor was an expressive man. He had looked prideful passing over the phone, but as he watched Jan look at the photo she saw his face wilt. He seemed as though he thought of happiness as behind him, or as something belonging to children.

"Did I tell you Anna paints? And I'm a writer," said Jan. He handed back Victor's phone.

Victor nodded but did not answer. He seemed indifferent. "And you're a musician," Jan added. Again Victor nodded indifferently. After a while he excused himself, took a call outside in Spanish, and then went upstairs to sleep. Jan and Anna drank another glass each then said goodnight.

In autumn everybody sees the moon more often. The night regains its dominance.

She couldn't sleep. Anxiety was warping her. She went outside.

Tonight the moon looked like an enormous yellow bowl absorbing light from stars and seeping it out again, making the dark blue sky look almost greenish. The color drained as it rose until the sky was all black, but the moonlight was still shining on the orchard and in the duck pond, where it landed on the water like a waterlily. Its image fractured and reassembled itself. My life could be like that, she thought sleepily: like a heavenly body which fractures and reassembles itself. That's right. The waters of life are reorganizing.

Whenever the ducks swam in the pond their quacks sounded like sprung springs…beside it the fluffy mushrooms fruited up from their structures and the fibers of the cattails ballooned out like earthbound dustclouds. There were thick greengold algae ringlets in the water and fresh moss and lichen grew wetly on the rocks.

Such a pretty season and no time to admire it.

But maybe I can remember this scene for some future feeling. Some future project. Life-beneath-moonlight.

Humans trade stories with each other. That's life. That's the life I'm accepting.

She felt too nervous to go to see the apples. There was movement upstairs. No talking. Either Victor or Jan was stirring. She frowned. Something with Jan was already shifting in an unknown direction: whenever she asked him to do something he did it quicker, quieter.

She went back inside and with some difficulty blacked out.

There was no precipitating day for the harvest to begin, no gargantuan shift in her perception of the farm as though overnight it had changed from something-contemplated into something-productive. It was simply September 14, the tree leaves darkening; the fifteenth, their first day with Victor, then the sixteenth, the cold crisp air, Jan's red jacket, Victor impatiently awake before anyone else, the firewood in the stove, all the gear in the grass (crates, sharpies, pallets, ladders, picking bags, the utility trailer), the apples red and ready, the sun still rising, the fog on the hills, the crows. Sean arrived late in his Ford. He careened over the hill just as Anna picked a Ruby Beauty from the sea of red fruit, lifting the apple and twisting it, feigning assurance. It was a few minutes before eight o'clock.

"So sorry," he said, running up to them. He caught his breath. "Underestimated the drive." He held out his hand and smiled at them all with round red cheeks. He was long-limbed, gangly, like a monkey. "Sean."

She shook it, then sat down cross-legged in the grass and put the apple on the cutting board next to the kitchen knife and the iodine solution. She would test the apple for its starch content, just to make sure they were really ready to be picked, though the colors of the skin indicated they were. The men stood impatiently around her. The apple was an imperfect, beautiful thing. A bruise here and there. Gil had assured her that customers didn't mind it so much. Heritage apples endured visual imperfections in exchange for their purity: free of pesticides et cetera. Not far from Victor's friend's logic, she thought.

There were two crescent-moon bruises in the corner of the apple. She sliced it open.

The flesh was brown. It looked like mud. A fat maggot lay dead in the apple like a fossil.

"Gross!" cried Jan.

Sean looked horrified.

"It happens," said Victor. "The crescents mean bugs got to it."

He went to the row and picked another as Anna dropped the dead fruit in a bucket. Her hand was trembling.

Victor came back less assured. He handed her another apple. No bruises.

She cleaved it. This one was clean, yellow. A success! She brushed it with the iodine. She wanted to speak to it but the men stood around watching her in the fog.

"So what's the protocol here?" said Sean.

"We're starting at the south row, where all the equipment is," said Jan. "I'll show you how to pick them when we're there."

"I can't wait to see those big apples."

"The Ruby Beauties ripen first," said Anna. "So that's where we're starting."

"We can still walk over and see them, though," said Jan.

Anna felt her face twitch.

"What if they aren't ready?" said Sean. "Do I just go home?"

She hadn't thought of that. Anna looked at the starch chart on her phone. Back at the apple, back at the phone. She tried to see if the blue-black patterns would emerge on the face of the apple like a Rorschach test. But the yellow iodine just sat there.

She looked up at the kid and smiled.

"They're ready."

"Then let's get started," said Victor. He walked off to the ladders and the rest of them followed. This time, Jan and Anna worked beside each other on the row, and Sean and Victor were the ones who could be seen through the prison limbs of the trees. They made an odd pair. Victor in his fleece jacket and old boots had tucked a small radio into his large back pocket. He flipped between stations as they worked. The sound was sometimes distorted by static, or muffled and garbled by his denim pants. He was focused, quiet, listening. Sean in his very clean tennis shoes acted almost aggressively cheerful, smiling way too often but never with his eyes, which always seemed to be in pain. He seemed to be struggling with some secret psychic problem he hoped labor would resolve. He kept pausing to take sensitive photos of the landscape, the apples and the hills, framing them with his delicate fingers.

For that reason he kept falling behind the rest of the group. Victor sped ahead. The four of them were arranged like a hunter's bow.

"Put the phone away," Anna said softly.

Sean flinched, did so, and kept picking.

"Nothing wrong with an affinity for nature," Jan said.

Anna watched Sean with restored calm. He was concentrating on the smooth retrieval of the apples from their branches—what few hadn't been picked off, on his side, by Victor. Jan went to him and reached through the leaves.

"You could afford to snap a picture or two if you pick them a little faster." Jan made a violent twisting motion in the air. "Trust the technique. Snap its neck!"

"I'd rather you pick them slow," Anna interjected again.

Sean nodded. Jan silently rejoined Anna's side. Victor seemed not to hear.

With a rhythm finally established she tried to tune out the others and feel the orchard as she worked. She was experienced at this meditation from working with Jan. But was it possible at this pace? The work was hard, she was already sweating, there was no time for stillness, and the picking bag attached to her body grew heavier and heavier like a pregnancy. She held a Ruby Beauty in her hand and Jan made a joke about Malevich in the fields. She smiled tightly. It was funny. Sean relayed an anecdote about an art history class he'd taken at school but hadn't understood. She shared an eyeroll with Jan then turned the apple around in her palm. Bruised again. She dropped it. She twisted another off like a lightbulb, accidentally breaking off the spur. Her heart was beating fast so she paused, before inspecting it, to look out at the trees. To steady herself. Even among a single cultivar, she was faced with the iconoclasm of each apple, like birds perched upside-down on the bottom of the branch, fat red cardinals, oversaturated flamingoes, mottled pigeons. An aviary of apples. The trees were floral, fragrant, cloying.

Surely this apple would be unblemished. She turned it over. It was bruised too.

The air was sliced by Victor's tinny rock music and the endless plopping of apples falling from Victor's hands.

"What are you doing?" she asked.

He glanced up at her without pausing. "Each tree seems worse," he explained.

What was that expression on his face? Embarrassment?

She started working faster and saw that it was true. In this section, around one in every three or four apples were undamaged. She found a ripe one but accidentally bruised it from squeezing it too hard. That was okay. She dropped it in her bag.

She tried to convince herself not to worry, remembered Gil saying organic orchards lost more fruit than others, the apples would sell at a premium to offset the loss…she even tried to enter into their grotesqueness, to feel it. She wasn't above the grotesque. But her mind kept flattening out images into those simple and dismal calculations: the number of trees, the fruit per tree, the salvageable fruit per tree, the price per bushel. And the heavy feeling like an iced-over ocean: an ocean that had iced over while she wasn't looking.

It was Jan who kept a sick account of the damaged fruits, showing off the worst apples to Anna almost sadistically. The danger was not real to him. At any rate, he'd always been the type to laugh through disasters. Though he always claimed to do it out of a kind of existential astonishment, it only made him seem more impervious than ever to the blows of the world.

Index of Ruin

1.

A smallish apple picked by Jan with an enormous black hole the color of pure night in its lower half. It was being invaded by two sleek wasps which had taken over the apple and made it their cave. She tried to think about this symbolic development step by step, how she'd stroked the bumblebee in spring on the apple flower, and now the wasps were glaring out at her from their black cave of rot…no, no connection. Wasps aren't bees. Forget it.

2.

Victor found this one. It was half-eaten, the white flesh of a Ruby Beauty oxidized into a vomitlike yellow-brown color. Little pecks around the calyx. Sean said it was probably a grackle, because he'd once seen one swoop down to eat his discarded apple. Grackles loves apples. Grackles love apples, he kept saying, kind of giggling, repeating the rhyme. Jan said that didn't prove anything. Anna looked at the dozens of little bites on the fruit. Not the big cleaving bite of human molars: the small feasts of pests. Death by a thousand cuts!

3.

Another of Jan's, black as the first. In its darkness like ripples on black water were gray warping concentric circles. Some kind of mold? She was afraid to touch it. She was disgusted. She felt like vomiting. The circles looked like they might crumple under her finger like charcoal. But there was not the same inhuman holy cleanness of a fire: the apple was alive and wet with bugs and fungus…those circles were cognizant. Were they even moving? They were gazing right back at her. Around the black pool, the apple's orangish flesh was wrinkled like earth deformed by an earthquake. She flipped the apple around. This side was smooth, red, perfect. Back again. The disfigured side rippled like fabric, as though sloughing off skin.

4.

Anna found an apple tucked up against a bird's nest. It might have even been supporting it, and if the thin stem was severed the nest would break apart. She decided not to pick it, even though the nest seemed abandoned.

Not everything is about money, she thought deliriously. Some things are about love, she thought, justifying something. Brown bumps were bubbling up from the bottom of the apple. Brown bumps with black pinpricks in their center like a swollen wound.

5.

Sean picked up a crushed apple on the ground. Anna tried to look severe as he shimmied through the leaves to show it to Jan. She tried to see the apple. With that huge cavity in its side, you could look down into the apple like a deity looking into a cave carved into ruby-red rock. A cave like some animal's den. Who had taken shelter here? A little field mouse? A centipede? Emerging in the morning, sticky, continuing a journey through the rotten red hills, well-rested like a traveler who has taken shelter from the desert or the snow by gutting his mount and sleeping in its eviscerated stomach…that's right. If you're a small thing, moving through the windfall is like walking through the rot of a battlefield.

She couldn't take it anymore! She abandoned her ladder in the grass and went to look at the other rows. It was the same with the Federations and Teratourgimas, though here and there she could find one nearly pristine tree. The blight was concentrated at the orchard's center. She'd known the trees weren't perfect, knew some of them were bound to rot, but perhaps now that she was really looking, not friendly but wanting (or was it always wanting?), not pretending to see but really seeing, she noticed how many of them looked so evil…the blackened leaves and apples on the Teratourgimas were especially disgusting, the way their largeness accentuated their rot.

Her workers—because that's what they are to me, she thought, aren't they?—were slowly filling up the crates. She came back to make sure. Then she dashed through the rows to find the Alice cultivar she had grafted in the spring. It had seemed so sickly, and part of her was certain the evil little thing had infected the other trees, and that if she unearthed it she could pull out the sickness through the root system, the sickness would look like rotten tendrils tangling itself up with the mycorrhiza, and if she kept pulling gingerly, so as not to break it, the blight would seep out of the apples, the leaves, and the bark of the infected trees. Like extracting a worm from a body…the bugs would vanish and the sweet cream-colored sugars would emerge like the substance of angels.

But it wasn't a villain. It was just a little plant. Using her pocketknife she extracted it from the earth easily. And the rest of the trees remained, broadcasting their malevolence.

She tossed the sapling in the grass and walked back to the men.

They had moved some distance down the row. Anna maneuvered through the trees to reach them, walking carefully around the apples they'd tossed in the grass. Sean and Victor were still picking on their ladders and seemed to alter themselves as she approached. How, she couldn't tell. Stiffer, quieter. Jan was collecting some of the discarded apples in a spare bucket.

"What do you want to do?" he said.

"Keep picking. The good ones can't just rot on the trees. I'm going to call someone."

Jan nodded. He kept standing beside that disgusting bucket.

"Keep picking," she repeated. *Get back on the damn ladder*, she wanted to say.

Jan dropped the apple he was holding into the bucket, shiny and deep red, whose small ring of infection looked like corroded metal on a garnet orb. He glared.

Back inside Anna felt the cabin was smaller and more oppressive than ever. As if shadows had stained it from within. She rifled through some of Joe's records, pulling notebook after notebook off his bookcase. He had been the type of old man to write out website links by hand. His handwriting looked shaky, feeble on the yellow paper: nothing like the steadfast and self-assured man Tamara had depicted. Finally she found something that looked useful: some information for a research laboratory at the university's plant science department which offered fruit damage assessments. She called the number. The coordinator told her they'd stopped booking over the phone years ago, and she would have to fill out a form online. So she went to the website and did so, reporting the number of trees in the orchard, the names of the sprays she had used, the cultivars, what damage from previous years she could ascertain from skimming through Joe's records...when she was done her eyes stung from staring at the screen. She went out to pick more apples.

That night was the first night she dreamed of money. Or rather lay awake not dreaming, staring at the ceiling and watching the abstract lines of the wood grain materialize into bushels, watching beyond them the paradise of isolation construct its invisible gates and lock itself. Because if Jan hadn't arrived I wouldn't have lapsed, she thought. The apples wouldn't be strangers to me, enemies. I wouldn't have stopped looking. In the future there could be no compromise. But first I have to make enough money to make it through the year.

Her heart was pounding in her throat. She wasn't callous. She didn't need to rake it in. She didn't care about money in and for itself, like others. She wasn't like that. She only wanted to regain her solitude, feel again the pure divine lonely spring wind. The divine and the abstract, the gaseous: she saw it solidify into crates of apples. The work was melting its veneer of animal intimacy, but it could be reformed. Money was the formless thing that would reenable that intimacy...she was confusing herself. Money was finally appearing to her as something-tangible, or rather, an abstraction that could lead to the tangible, instead of as the distant imperative of her former bosses...now it was her imperative.

They salvaged what they could. At night Jan made bonfires.

Tonight he was frying something on a skillet while the rest of them sat around.

She liked the smell of fire burning and sat very close to it, basking in the heat on her face. She liked smokesmell in her hair and on her clothes. But beneath it she felt nauseous. There was nothing to do but wait.

"I'm having a lot of fun," said Sean.

She glanced at him through the smoke. Sean was crouching near the fire, warming his hands, eager to enjoy his tangential encounter with a different mode of life. This is the real world, a real world, his face seemed to say, a world different than the one I know, and he waited for her response with a look of rapt attention, a kind of perverse excitement. He was clueless.

"I like being in the fields."

"It's nice to be outside, isn't it," Jan offered.

Victor made a quiet sound she couldn't parse. He was tossing Pell sticks in the darkness.

Jan handed Sean a plate. "It's like meditating. If you're anything like me, focusing deeply on one thing at a time is what will keep you sane. No chasing butterflies."

Butterflies was Jan's word for inattention, life without purpose—something his family had once accused him of, Anna remembered, and which he had repurposed with a delightful irony. Usually he articulated it as a good thing. She watched him give Victor his plate.

"Anna will be fine," he said to Sean. "She always is."

Sean smiled and looked at her. She frowned and looked at Jan.

"You have no idea," she said obliquely.

Jan flinched. His cheek was painted orange by the fire. He kept talking to Sean.

"She's lying. I worked hard all summer. Don't mind her."

Victor kept eating. Furtively he glanced back and forth between Jan and Anna. Sean was looking morosely into the flames.

"I can't just take off any time," she said. She backed away from the fire but her face was still hot. "Like you."

Silence. Jan handed her a plate. She looked down on it. From above her came a green flurry of ripped-up cilantro, tossed onto her food. Like all of you, she thought with cruelty.

"Well, Anna, I won't just take off. Don't worry," he said. "And that's what matters."

She looked up at Jan. A defusing expression, an excessively friendly smile, the puppy-look he always gave whenever he was hurt.

She didn't smile back at him. They ate the rest of their meal without speaking.

The pomologist came Friday. It was the day before her first farmers market. She was alone with Victor in the packing shed, grading what fruit they had saved and watching as the bins of apples suitable for sale filled up miserably slowly, slower than grass grows, slower than suns rise. The pallets holding the bins were pretty and weathered: gray-brown with subtle shades of pink, blue, and green staining their planks. She tried to enter into them, see the apples on the pallets as coagulated orbs of color, see the repeated rotation of the fruit, something, but whenever she mounted the forklift to haul a full bin onto the utility trailer she just repeated the same dismal calculations: at $2.50 per pound, these 350 pounds of Federations will net $875 if they all sell, minus Sean's and Victor's wages...her real hope lay in the Teratourgimas at the northern end of the orchard, where Jan and Sean were now picking. Then they would start again at the first row of Ruby Beauties. She squinted out at the orchard, trying to see or hear them. She couldn't.

What she did hear was a sputtering engine, the crackling sound of pebbles displaced by tires. She looked and saw a car approaching. Without a word she went out to greet the scientist. When he exited his car, she was already beside it.

"Hi," the man said, offering his hand. "I'm Derek."

She shook it but forgot to offer her name. Her palms were sweating.

"Do you want water, tea, coffee?"

"No, thank you. I don't have much time today."

He went to his trunk and retrieved a large white canvas bag bearing the university's name, not unlike the picking bags, and a clipboard.

"You know how this works?"

"No."

"Based on the layout of your orchard, we pick ten apples from fifty trees, more or less at random, varying location and cultivar, and take them back to the university for analysis."

"You take them?"

"Yes," he said. "We have our students practice on them. If I assessed them off the spur, this would all be a lot more expensive."

He closed his trunk, then moved his torso back and forth, stretching off the feeling of being in a car.

"Could you bring me a ladder?"

She went. The price hadn't seemed cheap to her, and she began to wonder if the fruit she might lose in profit—150 apples—might not have been worth the extra money to have them assessed on the tree. Though that was only if they were all fit for sale, she thought miserably…she passed Victor, who glanced up at her and nodded. She didn't pass Sean and Jan. Where were they? They should have finished with the Teratourgimas by now.

Better just to do it. She returned with two ladders.

They entered the orchard. Derek pointedly stepped over a pile of sheep shit while walking into a row of Ruby Beauties. He waved flies from his body. He looked around at some of the scorched-looking branches as they walked. Then he stopped, it seemed to her, at a random tree.

"Not a lot of fruit on these."

"We've already done a first pass."

"Still." He set his ladder in the crook of a low branch, stepped onto the first rung, picked an apple, and dropped it into his bag. She noticed it was one of the apples with concentric circles. She was unsure if he'd seen it. Should he have taken a concentric one? She set her ladder against a branch on the opposite side of the trunk. Better find a clean apple for control, she thought, something less embarrassing.

"I'd prefer you didn't pick any," he said. "It has to be random. You understand?"

She stared at him. Her mind was elsewhere. Was that Jan and Sean in the distance? She thought she heard their laughter ringing over the hills.

No, of course not. They were too far away.

Everyone was always laughing. What was there to laugh about?

"You can go back to work," he said, looking a bit uncomfortable. "I'll come find you when I'm done. You were in your packing shed, right? Grading today?"

Behind him the trees were like a long tunnel. A long green throat of trees. Oh God, she thought, dizzy.

"Yes," she said. "All right."

She obeyed.

And as she walked back to the packing shed she felt the pleasurable flash of feeling, the violent burst of feeling, that the trees were a faceless green, that's right, she still wasn't above the grotesque, the grotesque pressing her in on both sides, lifting themselves to show the horrors of the fruit as a woman might lift up her dress, smelling like perfume, not woodsy or rustic but sickly, a compressed sugar-smell almost like packaged candy, like candy on the breath of thousands of children which were the apples. Young abominations, she thought with love and humor, and I am too. What happened? Perhaps it is I who have impressed myself on them, not the other way around—I who have imbued myself, my coldness, my failure, my rot. There was a pleasure in that. I've deformed things. By being here I've ruined them. She smiled deliriously, stepped over the sheep shit again, and returned to work.

But in the packing shed Victor was waiting for her.

He set down his apple when he saw her. "I found something you want to see."

He took her to the equipment shed. Clouds of dust billowed out of the ground, surfaces. The pull-chain light Victor drew lit up the room yellow and incomplete. It was just above a stack of pallets, spiderwebby, only recently revealed as they had begun using pallets. Victor squatted and pointed to it. A stone crack in the foundation.

"Looks pretty bad to me," he said.

"Does it?"

"You don't want horizontal cracks." He made a long horizontal line with his hand. "It happened to a farm I worked at in Washington. They tore the shed down."

After paying the pomologist, registering for the farmers market, accounting for wages…she couldn't possibly hire a contractor to fix a shed.

"We'll reinforce it ourselves tomorrow."

Victor paused. His face was hard as steel.

"It looks…" he said, lowering his eyes. "I don't know."

She didn't answer. For Anna, the pressing thing was the dilapidation of the farm, and the necessity of restoring a piece of a piece of its untouchedness. She tried to keep a straight face. She was keeping the unfolding cataclysm of the orchard close to her. None of the men had talked much about it directly. It was as if by silencing it it wasn't happening. Everyone else had his mission. Jan was renewing himself. Victor was making money. Sean was taking his break from school. Anna was handling the end of the world.

Meanwhile Victor's look of annoyance finally buckled into the word: "Fine."

He went back into the packing shed. She followed.

His look hadn't fazed her. She hadn't understood. Instead she paused to feel the chill on her spine, tried to calm herself, thinking: How much money I can make all depends on the consumer. The consumer. Ha-ha.

In the packing shed a new hardness calcified the air. No longer was Victor interested in making small talk about their work, the news, food, and whatever other innocuous topics could pass through the workspace like wind-in-grass. The air was short and hostile. The roof felt low and dark like a cave. And when Jan's and Sean's voices appeared, blowing into the shed before their bodies, their muffled laughter heightened by contrast the tension in the packing shed. But when they finally arrived with their crates full of Teratourgimas, whisking dead red and brown leaves in off the wind of their shoes, they grew silent, too.

Why? She looked at them. They didn't look back.

Victor smiled harshly over at Jan and nodded his head.

Are they plotting something? Of course not. What's there to plot? Do they pity me?

Maybe. She was furiously embarrassed, paranoid, dizzy. She glared at them all.

"Let's get as many of the Teratourgimas as we can graded and loaded before tomorrow," she announced. Her voice was low and it boomed through the room. "Victor, drop the Federations. Jan, Sean, put up your ladders."

They did as they were told. She got an apple from a crate. Here it was, untouched and undisfigured by ice: a Teratourgima. So big you almost needed two hands to hold it. So big it looked like an elephant's heart. This time she didn't want to take a bite. This was the legendary apple which would elevate her above all the others at the market, which would surround her with a kind of sparkling allure as well as a higher profit margin. She turned one around in her hand. This one was perfect! As before she admired its enormity, this time not for its poetic qualities, but for its useful, material ones. It was not the heavenly bigness of mountains, oceans, megafauna. She liked its bigness the way one likes a bigger bed. A bigger car. A bigger house.

She liked its bigness for what it could get her.

She rolled the apple into a bin and picked up another one.

Just a little flyspeck: gray-brown stains, purely cosmetic. She rubbed some of it off with her sleeve. Then she rolled the apple into a bin and picked up another one.

Part of this apple had collapsed in on itself. The collapsed portion looked liquified, like a pit of oil. She flinched at it. Not a good one.

She stood with it in her hands. The world was silent.

Then she heard the thumping of the men's apples and realized she had slowed down. She glanced up at them. In between apples, Jan was looking at her with soft interest, and, catching her eye, he smiled in a curious, polite way.

She scowled and held up her apple to the men.

"How did this one get picked?" she said. Accidentally, her voice came out with electricity. To make up for it she tried to look all around and smile at everybody, fluttering her eyelashes. It didn't make things better. They flinched, murmured, and made excuses.

She looked down and restarted with greater speed. They worked in silence until Derek returned. He tapped on the post of the shed by way of knocking.

He and Anna walked a few paces away from the shed and stood together in the grass. He had only his clipboard. The fog of the day was lifting and the colors were watercolor-light.

"Well, I'm done," he began.

"Great."

He took a deep breath.

"You'll get the full results by Monday evening, Tuesday at the latest, but I can tell you what it looks like to me."

"Okay."

"Most organic orchards are going to see a bit of everything. Scab, sooty blotch, lepidopterous moths—well, I don't have to list them for you. That all looked standard. What I saw massive amounts of were curculio-infested apples and fireblight-infested apples and branches. Do you know what those are?"

"Yes."

He wrote something on his clipboard.

"For the curculio, you might have missed a kaolin spray. Use Surround next year."

"All right."

"As for the fireblight, could be anything," he said with something in his voice. Pity? she wondered again. But she was happy to be pitied by this one. There was something soothing to his pity. "A bad thunderstorm, hail, pruning without sterilizing, even pollinators can spread it."

"I see."

"Our department has fruit-growing classes, and lectures, year-round…Maybe after the harvest you could sit in on some," he said gently. "The winter classes use persimmons, but you should still find some of it useful. Hopefully you'll have better luck next season."

Her throat constricted. She stared at the grass.

He seemed to want to go on, but he stopped himself.

They stood there stiffly. Laughter again from the packing shed.

She tried to eavesdrop on them, but she couldn't hear.

Derek shifted his weight.

"Well," he said.

"Sorry. How do I pay you?"

"We'll send an invoice, or if that's inconvenient, by check."

"Let's do check."

He followed her to the cabin. She'd been sure to get a checkbook in preparation for her new life at the farm, back when the idea of commerce had an abstract grace about it. A feeling of presiding over something, of stewardship. She had imagined signing her name in midnight black ink for a dozen dwarf apple trees, transporting them like a motorback forest, planting them in the wet earth, mingling things...

She had to fumble around in the desk drawer to find it. She grew more and more flustered as he waited. I must look so unprofessional...When she found it, it was so fresh-looking against the half-empty pens and yellow notebooks she used more often. He said to make it out to the department. When she gave it to him, he took it rigidly in his hands, like a claw clamp. He deformed the paper.

"Thank you," he said. "As I said, I'm in a hurry." He nodded. "Good luck."

He left.

She slouched down in her chair by the computer. It felt nice inside. She liked it inside. It was cool and dim. She liked it cool and dim. The way a mammal likes a hole. She looked dully at the stained glass lamp: autumn colors captured and refined. Then she looked out the window at the trees before looking away, embarrassed. It felt like the world was backwards: petalfall was the thing-reaped, the thing to celebrate, idyll, pink gentleness, while the actual harvest of the apples, the production and sale of the fruit, was preparation for...what? As though the pleasurable weight of promise was the promise itself. The dreaming is always nicer. Was that it? That's it. And even that second dream, that idle summer with Jan...she was on the verge of something, wasn't she?...

But the door banged open again. She looked. Bright light from the open door, overrunning the dimness of the cabin. Jan.

He appeared to her like a stranger. She narrowed her eyes. But it seemed she didn't to him, because he walked up to her, leaned against the desk, and put his large hand on her shoulder.

"Need a break?" he said. "Me too. You weren't kidding when you said it was hard. It's not even sixty degrees and I'm sweating."

She brushed his hand off her shoulder and scooted the chair away from him.

"No. I was just thinking."

"Sit there a minute."

He went into the kitchen. She heard him open the fridge and get something. He came back with a plastic yellow pitcher, sweet-smelling. He gave it to her. She looked at it. She looked up at him. Then, with a start, he went back to get a glass and handed that to her, too.

She kept looking up at him.

"Anna," he said. "Cider! I tried the press out last night. I couldn't sleep."

"What have you done?" She set the cider down carelessly and it spilled a little by the keyboard. "The cider-grade apples are for a brewery. I have to deliver them tomorrow morning."

"No, I chilled some of the unusable apples after chopping off the rotten bits. We were going to make some cider, remember? It's not alcoholic, but you can't have it all. I want some too." He winked at her. "Taste it."

She looked down at it, disgusted, remembering the liquid black flesh. But then she picked it up and took a sip. It was smooth and sour. Maybe a pleasurable sourness? Is this tartness? She had never particularly liked apples, at least not in a consumptive way.

"Tastes all right, doesn't it?" he said. "If we order some plastic jugs we can package and sell them through the winter. That way fewer apples will go to waste."

"Does that seem ethical?"

He leaned forward so his face was near hers. He smiled and rolled his eyes, like the two of them were in on some secret.

"But doesn't it taste all right?" he said softly. "You always loved sweets. Sweet-tooth."

She took another sip to hide her face from him. It did taste all right. "We could mull some, too," he went on in his normal tone. He sounded far away again. The sip became a gulp. Her whole field of vision was of the brown-red cider and the thick ring at the bottom of the glass. It was delicious! The flavor was fresh, sharp, and complex, despite the fruit it had come from. She'd acclimated to the taste. Nothing seemed rotten about it. And as she lowered the glass, there was Jan's face again, watching her with that same intensity. Something strange about his eyes. His hand was extended toward her face slightly, as though he were about to tilt her chin back to make her drink more. She scooted back again. He reached out and took the half-drunk glass from her hand, the way one takes a glass from a child, letting his fingers touch hers. He set it by the pitcher on the desk.

"I'll take that as a yes. Let me borrow your card, I'll order us some plastic jugs," he said, fluidly, going on so as to brush the fact aside: "I'll start thinking of a label design we can print. Then we'll eat lunch and finish up our work in the packing shed. How does that sound?"

She nodded. He'd saved her. Value-added products. That's how farms survive.

She felt deferent, full of gratitude.

"Jan, I'm sorry if I've been off," she mumbled.

His hand on her shoulder again, this time rubbing her with his thumb. "Anna, it's all right. We take care of each other."

Jan hadn't disagreed, which disturbed her. She had wanted him to say she'd been normal. She took out her wallet from the drawer and gave him her credit card. She watched him climb up to his room with a hollow feeling in her stomach. An emptied-out feeling. Just as he said, he came back down a few minutes later to get started on lunch. He was humming. It was not yet noon.

15

She woke up with a tightness in her chest and went immediately to the packing shed. Jan, Sean, and Victor were busy preparing what fruit crates they had not loaded the night before. When she arrived the three of them were chatting and lounging by the forklift.

"All ready," Jan said.

"Thank you."

She began to leave, already unthinking, but Jan stopped her.

"Anna, before you go, I want to run a label design idea by you," he said. He made a parting gesture with both hands as though clearing space for his vision. "Victor and I were talking about it. 'Lone Painter Ciders,' a woman collapsed like Arthur's Cleopatra, spirals for eyes like she's on acid and four paintbrushes between her fingers. We could print it in four colors, make it pop."

Her body tightened. She looked at Victor.

"Victor suggested the paintbrushes," Jan said. There was some edge in his voice.

"I really don't care," Victor said. He seemed annoyed to be involved. "I just said something so he'd shut up."

Anna looked at Jan. He was projecting one of his aggressively neutral looks: no way to know what was going on in there.

"Oh, come on," he said without changing. "Anna, it's just an idea."

She noticed Sean trying not to laugh in the corner.

"It would look great," Jan said.

"Let's get the crates loaded."

"Sure. After that, what would you say if we picked 'til noon and took the rest of the day off? Victor says he has some errands to run in town. I'll give him a ride then stop by the stand."

All three men were looking at her, variations on waiting-faces: Jan's playful sardony, Sean's bewildered curiosity, Victor's flat impatience. They looked like a painting. Anna felt her jaw tighten.

"Sure," she said eventually.

An ease broke out among the men.

"Thanks," said Jan. "Good luck today. And listen, I'm half-kidding."

Happy when she was finally alone, driving into town. It was a bluecool morning. She hung one arm out the window as she drove. She watched the wildflowers blur in the dawn, let herself think of nothing. A few crates of fancy-grade apples went to Prism Foods, the health food store; a few crates of cider-grades to Black Pond, the brewery. She got to a hardware store right when it opened and bought bricks and mortar mix. Finally she drove to the market. She opened the vendor map on her phone. She found her name and place.

The street was a tunnel of early color. Everywhere people unloaded vegetables, fruits, flowers, eggs, and preserves from their trucks and trailers. Lots of happy talk. The road was old red cobblestone, not far at all from the university. She could see its clocktower, the terraced flowerbeds of turtleheads and black-eyed Susans. She smiled. She felt oddly soothed. The canopy tent was already set up for her, flapping in the wind. Beneath it stood a folding table and a plastic chair.

She filled her table with baskets and her baskets with fruit, organized by cultivar. She put the Teratourgimas in the middle so they could dominate the center of the image. She unrolled the blue masking tape, stuck a piece haphazardly on the edge of the table beneath each cultivar, and wrote her prices down in black sharpie. She set up her kitchen scale and plugged in the card reader.

Now to wait.

All around her the other vendors draped huge colorful tarps bearing their farms' names and logos, their websites, over their folding tables and along the tops of their tents. She wasn't familiar with any of them. Some sold tote bags and even T-shirts. Others tiered their products vertically, with complex stands and kitschy signs bearing recipe ideas and suggestions on how to use their products. Advertisements for herbalist's workshops, canning workshops, social events…photographs of glass-jarred preserves and their motherfruit beside them.

None of this bothered her. She knew she could never degrade the orchard in that way. She trusted wholly the reputation of the Teratourgimas, the inbuilt clientele she would retain from Joe's stand, and above all the elegance of her approach. Because she had the dim idea that something about her stand would mysteriously attract people: its seriousness, its austerity. That something of the orchard's uniqueness would be communicated psychically.

But when she saw the tent for Pleasant Hill Orchard across from her, her heart did sink a little, and seeing their crates of fruit apple jams, apple butters, apple vinegars, apple ciders…she hadn't expected to be near another apple orchard.

Crouching on her chair like a cat she squinted at them. They either didn't see her or avoided her gaze. Two young farmers, or workers. They were laughing and chatting and writing out their prices in pink chalk on blackboards by their stands.

Fuji? Come on. And what the hell is a Cosmic Crisp?

The clock tower rang. Rustic. She looked at her phone. Noon.

She wasn't an idiot. Signs like that commanded attention. Why else would people subject themselves to them? A busy student whisking through the market on a day off from school would see Pleasant

Hill's cartoon sun smiling out from behind the poorly drawn hill, find it charming, think subconsciously how much she was enjoying the sunshine, the autumn, how nice it was to be out in the cool day, and go over there to buy the Fujis. Those were the kinds of people who bought more produce than you could possibly eat in a week. But wasn't there something irresistibly quaint about a lone woman and a crate of apples? As though your mother had set them down before you on the kitchen table. Anonymous and benevolent. Your mother doesn't come with signs. We all make compromises.

So she stood up from her chair with the anxious hesitancy of a newborn horse.

"Apples," she called weakly.

Nobody…

"Huge apples," she called a little louder.

The school's blue-and-gold banner hung dead in the air from the lamppost. The din of the market made her feel lonely, as though everyone around her was speaking a foreign language.

But it had only been a few minutes.

She cupped her hands around her mouth.

"Apples, fresh apples! Come and buy some apples, fresh from the farm."

The words felt wicked on her tongue. She kept standing and shouting the phrase. She tried to look at everyone at once, not as individuals, but the way one looks at a line of ants or a field of grass. The young farmers at Pleasant Hill Orchard were looking at her and talking to each other. She pretended not to notice.

Then she made eye contact with a man with a boy on his arm. With desperation she tried to establish a taut, invisible line between her and them. It was time to reel him in. She pulled her mouth into an artificial smile. Is that how you do it? Is that him looking guilty and inconvenienced as he walks my way, dragging the boy who must be his son behind him? Her eyes dropped. The apples look like red tumors today.

"Hello," she said when he arrived.

He smiled tightly and nodded without looking at her. "Hi," he said.

He made a gesture like he'd like to browse in peace. Fine by her. His hand hovered just beneath his gaze as he looked at the cultivars. The boy's tiny face was just peeking up over the table. The man picked up an apple. It was a Ruby Beauty. He considered it and set it back down.

Then, gently, holding himself at a respectable distance away from the tent, his face dappled by the sun-through-leaves while Anna watched him from the shade, he tried to pick up one of the Teratourgimas, fumbled, then caught the apple with both hands, chuckling to himself.

Time to engage. She leaned forward.

"Grotesquely enormous apples, aren't they?" said Anna.

The man blinked twice.

"Sure, they're pretty big!" he said, blushing, and meanwhile Anna's body fluttered with this new electric current of fear and excitement they call—yes, that's exactly what it was—the thrill of the sale.

But after pretending to consider them for a moment longer, the man thanked her and hurried away.

The day went on. She did better. She called again:

"Apples, fresh apples! Come and buy some apples, fresh from the farm!"

Always the same phrase. She grew numb to the wicked feeling. Now when people approached, she nodded at them and let them shop. She was imitating the old farmers with nothing to prove. Whenever someone asked which cultivar she recommended, she tried to think about what it was people liked about fruit, and asked:

"Sweet or tart? Firm or soft?"

And then guided them. Many walked lightmindedly up to her

stand to buy apples without really looking at them, rotely checking "apples" off their shopping lists, their arms draped with tote bags. One young woman came up to her and immediately bought a single Federation, and, standing in front of the boxes of apples as though before a field of red flowers, took a huge hungry bite of it and marveled aloud how it didn't taste like pesticides, how there was no red dye seeping into the flesh, how she'd never lived anywhere with a farmers market and how she'd thought she'd hated apples until trying what her roommate had bought last week. I wasn't here last week, Anna almost said, but stopped herself, and, feeling deceitful, sold her three pounds of fruit.

When the woman left, Anna saw one of the Pleasant Hill farmers, a woman, looking right at her. Now that their eyes had met, the woman weaved through the crowd to say hello.

"Hi, I don't think we've met," she said. She smiled. "I'm Casey."

"Anna. Nice to meet you."

They shook hands.

"You run the farm that used to be a factory, don't you?" said Casey.

"No. It was a nature preserve."

"Sorry. I mean before. Right?"

Casey looked down at the Teratourgimas, pressing her lips. Anna studied her. She looks a bit like me, she thought. The resemblance made her uneasy.

"I don't know," she said.

"Gadwall Orchard?" Casey pressed. "Used to be run by an old guy?"

Anna tried not to answer, but Casey noticed and seized on her flash of recognition.

"That's right, isn't it?"

"That's right."

"We always loved his apples," she said. "He gave us some Teratourgima trees a few years ago. This is our first year selling them.

Hope they hit!" Toothy smile. Casey had a childish gap between her teeth. "Has he retired, then? Are you leasing?"

She felt hot and nauseous, then the breeze came. She'd looked at those apples. The woman was lying. There were no Teratourgimas at her stand.

"I need to sell a bit more before the market ends," said Anna. "Do you mind?"

"Of course. Sorry. It was great to meet you."

But the end of the day was slow. People passed her stall without even seeing her. Pleasant Hill didn't get much business either. Everyone had finished shopping.

"Sunday's usually busier," Casey shouted during a dead moment. Her voice flowed with friendliness. The man beside her nodded in agreement, as did the woman at the stand to the left of them, who was all sold out of pastries.

Anna smiled but her eyes were dead. Maybe she would have to produce some marketing material after all. If none of us did, it wouldn't be like this, she thought with despair. We could all be pure. She hunched over her apples in the darkness of the shade.

Finally Jan arrived.

"Hey!" he shouted from behind the tent. It was nearly five.

"Where have you been?" she said. "Where's Victor?"

Jan sat down on the curb and splayed his feet out on the cobblestone.

"Sorry, I didn't know I would be so missed," he said. "I dropped Victor off at a bar after we finished his errands. Some dive on the west side of town, guess he knows some people there. I said I'd pick him up on the way home. As for me, I met up with Sean and his friends in the afternoon."

"You're friends now, are you?" Anna said.

"Yeah. The two of you would have a lot to talk about. He's

thinking of studying art. Or environmental science. He can't seem to decide, but I'm winning him over, don't worry."

Anna adjusted her baskets of fruit. She didn't answer.

"You're not mad about this morning, are you? I was teasing." He stood up and set his hand gently on her lower back. "You look exhausted. Let me try and sell some."

Exhausted, she agreed. For the final hour Jan took over reeling in the late afternoon stragglers, shouting with freshvoiced vigor. She took his spot on the curb and watched him. Business picked up. He was a natural salesman, charming, extroverted. Casey and the other Pleasant Hill farmer watched, but this time they did not approach. Anna glared at them from behind Jan's body.

At six they packed up. They went home separately. When she drove up the hill of the orchard it was sunset. Nobody home. She spent twenty minutes by herself. The light was lovely, like amber. Perfect sound of evening birds. She left the cabin door open to let the sound and color in. She breathed deeply.

But she didn't enjoy it long. Counting her cash at the kitchen table she found she hadn't made nearly enough money, even with what Jan had squeezed out of the last hour.

She threw the money down on the table. Useless.

Chicken and rice for dinner, Jan's pointless enumeration of the spices, a conversation between Jan and Victor about something she didn't care about, something Sean had said in the orchard, their opinions on him. She played with her fork and ate slowly. The cabin was orange, candles and shadows. Filled with the sound of the men's laughter.

"He needs to toughen up!" said Victor. "He's too old to be that sensitive."

"You're misunderstanding him," Jan said. "We were all like that once."

"Not at his age." Victor shook his head over and over. "Not me."

Jan went upstairs after dinner to get some writing done. I'll probably kick him out when winter comes, she thought, watching him climb the ladder into the dark. Start over.

The thought made her smile.

She stopped Victor as he was climbing up after him.

"I want to get started on the foundation," she said.

"It's night."

"I bought everything today. I won't be able to sleep for a few more hours."

Victor stayed frozen on the ladder. His muscles were rigid as branches. They could both hear Jan shuffling around upstairs.

Victor relaxed his body slightly and said, "It's not going to fall down tomorrow."

"Let's go ahead and get started."

After all, the days were for picking. To hide her frustration she turned around, went to the door, and opened it. She glanced back at him. He tensed up again. Slowly he climbed back down the ladder. She could hear every limb on every rung.

In the shed they mixed mortar in one of Joe's old wheelbarrows. The work hurt her muscles, already sore from picking. It was dim. The only light came from the yellow bulb on the pull chain. Around it hung darkness. Moths fluttered their wings gray as ash. They scraped long, wet, grainy smears of mortar. The night was calming her a little.

"Sorry if Jan's bothering you," she said between blocks. "He can be so…"

"No, I like him," Victor said without stopping.

He didn't elaborate and he didn't turn to face her. They kept working silently.

"So they tore the other shed down?" she tried again.

"Yes."

"Those cracks looked about the same?"

"Worse."

"That's good," she said. "Think you'll work for them again?"
"No."
She had scraped her hand on a brick. She paused to lick off the blood. A little dirt got in her mouth too. As they kept working the wound clogged up with mortar.
"Why not?"
Victor made a sound between a sigh and a grunt. For the first time he paused to wipe away the sweat.
"I'll never willingly work in the west again. It's nice and cool here," he said. "Nice cool nights."
They made it through three layers in two hours. By eleven they were exhausted.
"All right," she said. "Let's finish it tomorrow."
Victor set down his tools harshly. They clanged against a brick. Without a word he went back inside.
Exhausted and distracted, hoping for a better market tomorrow, she brushed her teeth for a long time. When she rinsed she spit blood.

A drowsy Sunday. The men stumbled out of the equipment shed holding their ladders like boys with pillows. Sean yawned, then so did Jan and Victor. It was foggy and warm. Nice to see how the weather changes, Anna thought. Its light, mist, wind. She couldn't wait for it to be like that again all the time: to wake up and receive no new information but the different weather each day. Silence will reign. All winter I'll sleep and recover, like the bear.
"Save more apples for cider today," Anna told Jan privately as the men entered the trees. "It's a good idea."
"You got it."
She was tired too, but somehow selling apples came easier that day. It really was busier. A thick swaying grove of people separated her from the stalls across the street. That was why it took her until the end of the day to see that Pleasant Hill Orchard was selling their

Teratourgimas, too, and that they were selling them for $8.25/lb.—a full dollar cheaper than hers.

Something burned in her as she tore down her stand. Who expects this kind of sabotage? How do people manage? Isn't this life for the soft of spirit? How much business had they stolen? She found herself wondering what their orchard looked like, if the crude cartoon sun-and-hill of their banner bore any resemblance to the land at all, if she'd ever known serenity or solitude—unlikely, just look at that bitch laugh—or if it was really just a business venture for them, a heartless means of turning a profit. And for what?

So when Casey showed up in front of her after she had almost finished packing up the unsold apples, Anna did not greet her.

"Anna," Casey said. "Some of us like to trade goods at the end of the markets to offset grocery costs. Are you interested? There's a couple more young farmers like us I'll introduce you to."

Anna didn't answer. She didn't even look. She lifted her last crate back onto the utility trailer. Casey was still standing there as Anna slammed the car door shut. Still standing there as she started the ignition. As she drove away.

Back at the orchard no one was in the packing shed. Sunset again, pink and orange sky. She brought the unsold fruits into the shade and went to the fields to go look for everyone. It was payday.

Deep within a Federation row, on the easternmost edge of the field, there was a small lean-to with a red roof. It looked like one of the structures Gil and Tamara used to house their sheep. She had never fully understood what it was for. When she had first arrived at the orchard, dead, overgrown, reserved, abandoned, it had contained a few plastic chairs and a few plastic buckets. She'd left them there.

That was where she heard the men. She approached from behind the structure and heard their voices mingling with the radio.

"This is insane," Jan said.

"Yes," Victor said. "Wait."

The men were quiet. A guitar riff rang out from the radio.

"That's what I like. That guitar. It sounds like a voice."

"Have you ever thought about playing again?" asked Sean.

A long exhale. "No."

"You ought to. Just something to play around the fire. Then you wouldn't be so moody."

Victor laughed slowly. "No, no. I don't know."

"I bet Anna would buy you one. You can get a cheap acoustic guitar for nothing."

"I don't want to do that," Victor said, suddenly serious.

"Hell, I'll ask her," said Jan. "And you can't stop me."

Quiet laughter. The song finished out and went to commercials.

"You were saying?" said Sean.

"That was all, really. She reminds me of him. It's interesting. Being here has given me a new perspective on the guy."

Someone's else's exhale, lightly pitched, maybe Sean's. Jan went on.

"You know, when I was a teenager, I used to get so annoyed when people would stop to take pictures of the sunset. It happens every night, I'd say, it's nothing special. I was such a brat! Look at those colors."

"I always liked the sunset," Victor said.

"Guess I was the only cynic," said Jan.

More laughter. Anna looked up. The painted world. You could take off like a dandelion into that color. Everyone else must have been looking too, because it was quiet except the radio.

A plastic chair creaked. After a while Sean seemed to think he'd been spoken to.

"Yeah," he said.

Anna turned the corner. There they were: Victor, Jan, and Sean, sitting in plastic chairs with their feet splayed out in the dirt. They were bifurcated by light and shade. Jan had a spliff in his hand:

sweet-smelling, mossy, slow smoke curling up into the roof. No wind today. He flinched when he saw her. He dropped the spliff on the ground.

"Anna," he said. "It's mine," he said quickly. "Sorry."

The men looked dazed: like they were seeing her through a dream. Anna bent down and picked a butt off the ground, shaking off the dirt. She picked up two more. She put them in her pocket. Is that a stain on the ground where it was? Like the earth had been scorched, violated.

"Victor, Sean, I have your money," she said.

She took out the money and counted their payment in two handfuls of ten- and twenty-dollar bills. Jan watched her hands. She angled her body away to count furtively.

The birds were chirping. No one spoke.

She handed Sean a stack of money, then Victor.

Both of them counted their stacks. She watched them severely.

Sean looked satisfied and stuffed the money in his pocket. But Victor looked up at her and just as she was saying:

"Break's over. I'll get a ladder. Let's pick another hour."

He said:

"This isn't enough."

Anna took out her phone and showed him the spreadsheet, which displayed how many bins they'd all logged and how many hours of packing and transporting apples they'd logged. She handed it to him. He took it, studied it for a moment, and handed it back.

"This is thirty short."

"Where?" she said harshly, squinting at the phone.

"I helped you last night with the foundation."

Anna paused, trying to think. The silence went on and on.

"Well," she started to say.

"Give him the money, Anna," Jan interrupted. "Goddamn."

She forked it over.

16

The world grew cold and dry. As they walked out to the fields to scavenge what was left of the apples Jan watched the brittle leaves crunch beneath his boots. Half of them had fallen and the honey locust pods were yellow and decaying in the earth. He was cold. With the first flood of the harvest over, Anna spent most of her time at the computer, leaving the rest of them to talk freely.

They had all sorts of topics to pass the time, memories, politics, food, the future, Jan's adventures, Victor's plans, Sean's puerile fear of entering the world—

"It doesn't really matter what you do," Jan said. "The world's going to shit anyway."

And yes, sometimes the boss, at which point the others would look to Jan, who shook his head and told them with a loyalty he was finding it increasingly difficult to justify: "She's not well."

Whenever she entered the orchard so did silence. Their limbs locked up, anticipating scrutiny. They listened to the radio and her intermittent orders. They felt her brown eyes. And when she left, their conversations reblossomed.

There was something skeletal about her. It was something he'd noticed from the moment he'd arrived and which had only worsened with time. It wasn't that she was thin or gaunt, and for as long as he'd known her she'd always had her episodes, but something in her affect made it seem like she was almost ecstatic in how she was barely holding on to life: like the alarmed, happy void of an animal skull's eye sockets. Her own eyes were given to a kind of endless wandering: they moved around voraciously as she spoke as if trying to eat up everything around her, or else they were completely immobile, like a statue's, not even moving to look down at her food, register conversation, watch where she was walking, looking at what? She bumped into things often and had started mumbling under her breath about her plans when she didn't think anyone else could hear: "New kinds of trees, I always loved almond flowers…and to bring the berry bushes to life…websites, banners and whatever else you do…a farm stand, pick-your-own, not crazy…"

There was no more twilight talk. After dinner they all separated. Jan did the dishes while Anna went out to work on the foundation. Victor went to bed early.

One night Jan went out to check on her and found her stooped over on her knees in the shed, pushing a brick slowly into the mortar, watching it squeeze out from underneath the brick like jelly on a sandwich.

"Need help?" he asked.

She scraped the trowel along the excess mortar, slow and loud, making a horrific raking scraping sound.

A moth near the yellow light was disturbed.

"No," she said quietly.

She didn't look back at him.

"You can always ask me," he said, with special emphasis on the last word. She kept working as if she could not hear him.

He went away.

A few days later he saw that Anna had a contractor with her, and the day after, two more. A new group of men arrived at the orchard: men who tore down the bricks she stacked and in time completed the job without her help. Victor laughed. He told Jan she was far from the craziest farmer he'd worked for.

Time went on. Deadness hung in the air. It landed on things. The trees looked dead. The grass looked dead. The harvest lasted twenty-four days. Afterward, though there was still fruit on the trees, neither Sean nor Victor could financially justify the time it took scavenging the branches to fill a crate. One sunny day in October it was time for Victor to move on. He bought himself a bus ticket toward spinach harvest several towns over.

They made their beds. Jan liked how the light from the window landed on their sheets, the way the dust motes floated around in the attic.

"You're all packed up?" said Jan.

"Yeah."

"Then let's go."

They climbed down the ladder. They stood there near the door, looking at Anna across the room, who was squeezing her knuckles one hand at a time as she stared at the computer.

"We're off," said Jan.

Anna turned her chair around to look at them.

The men let themselves be observed.

They looked exhausted. Victor was in his fleece jacket and Jan in his thick red one. Both had backpacks hanging off their shoulders. Jan's hung slimly down. He always carried his aging Chromebook and one or two library books. Victor's bag was enormous, green, covered in zippers. It contained everything he owned and it didn't even close all the way.

Anna nodded at them, raised a hand, forced a smile.

"Good luck" was all she could think to say.

Victor thanked her and nodded back. Jan smiled patiently. He walked out and Victor followed. She listened to their footsteps outside the door and the muffled resumption of their conversation. Jan's engine choked alive. She heard it run idly, then the sparkle of tires on the gravel.

Back to the computer. The girl at the market had said something about a factory, but it didn't make any sense. The orchard was so lush, so much life and fertile soil…there were no steel or metal objects in the ground, no anonymous ruined structures, nothing. She went to the register of deeds site for the county, an old website, baby blue and green design.

She searched for his name.

There was the recent paperwork she'd signed from his estate to hers. Before that, the deed from his own purchase in 2003. He'd registered the name "Gadwall Orchard" under his sole proprietorship—that's right, she remembered, because he'd bought it just after he was widowed. The handwriting on his signature had the same boxy letters as the notes in his files, but mediated through the screen it looked deader, lacked the smudged pen and the warm yellow of the notepads. As Tamara had said, the person he'd bought it from had inherited it, in 1987, and before that, from the mid-'70s to mid-'80s it had shuffled through a number of hands in the Ray family, whoever they were, always through a trail of death. The man who'd sold it to Joe had inherited it from his dead father, who had inherited it from his dead aunt, who had assumed sole ownership from her dead husband.

She crawled through names. She made sure she was looking at the right document by comparing the precise language of coordinates and landmarks, and the last sentence of the description, which always ended: "beginning and comprehending the same lands recorded in book 192 at page 331 of the Turtlehead County register of deeds, charted by William Cooper in 1913." There was no indication of any nature preserve, any factory, any prior use of the land at all: in fact she couldn't find any records before 1971.

She rubbed her lower back. That pleasurable soreness of the body had hardened into aches from picking and stooping with bad posture. She went to the kitchen to make coffee and passed the open door to her bedroom.

Midge raised her head and thumped her tail. Pell must have been outside somewhere.

In the summer the diffuse sunlight through the bamboo window made the room glow green like a glass kelp forest, but today there was a peculiar absence of color in the air, like it had been crystallized and frozen out of the sky. Bright, gray, almost brownish air, like the agouti fur of wolves. Is that how Burchfield would paint it? The wolf sky.

As the kettle heated she sat down on the kitchen floor. Stroking the dog, looking at the light. She felt a sad, sober sense of understanding…like she had found some shredded-up scraps of a person, colorful and unintelligible, recovered from the vortex of the internet.

The water whistled. She stood up slowly to make coffee then returned to the computer with her mug. She looked at the clock. 12:06.

The real question was money. There were a few options. In the long term, hope lay in the cider operation. In the short, there were loans. She could borrow money against the farm, throw the orchard into question…she felt tension in her spine. Her jaw clenched. There were standard FSA loans, but she lacked the requisite years of managerial experience or agricultural education…finally, there were microloans, with laxer requirements, though she would have appoint a "mentor" in lieu of pretending the orchard was profitable. Who could she ask? Gil, Tamara?

It had been some time since she'd seen them. She thought of Tamara's disapproving stare. She picked at her fingers, ripping off a dry bloody hangnail.

Gil wouldn't be opposed.

She went to his and Tamara's website. Sleek, modern. The wool flank of a Merino filled up her screen, with the words BUY WOOL DIRECT plastered on top of it.

Then the photo faded to the pinkish smiling face of one of the dairy sheep. TURTLEHEAD DAIRY CO-OP.

Next a photo of the flock roaming over green hills. It was taken in late afternoon. Tamara trailed behind them with a border collie. Gil's loving hand, she assumed, behind the camera. OUR PRACTICES. She squinted. She zoomed in. Pixelated, she could just make out a person she didn't know handling a sheep against one of the shelters, perhaps shearing it or treating it as Tamara had that day.

Pleasant Hill's website was plainer, less modern. She looked at others from the market whose names she had remembered. Dozens and dozens of farms.

She leaned back in the chair. She felt a blankness.

Within that blankness, an overabundance, like white noise.

Her red eyes were burning.

Is this who I thought I'd be? she thought suddenly, desperately. How do you extract something gently from the earth?

She closed the tabs. She sat there in front of the computer. She opened her email. There was the contractor's invoice, $5,780, including the cost to knock down her pitiful wall, which might have addressed the problem had it been less severe. Unlike the pomologist, no university deal. Nothing to be learned.

There was also Derek's report. He had been right about the main problems: curculio and fireblight. Some early cultivars were strangely underripe. He'd thanked her. Keeping track of pest patterns was useful for his department as well, he'd written. At the bottom of the email he attached a photo of his students smiling at the camera, happily dissecting her failed apples on black lab tables.

She looked at the apples in the photograph. To her a perfect apple was a red halo rotating, solidifying. A halo of red light. A perfect apple held no history, no genealogy, no ecology, no symbolism. It wasn't a product and it didn't appear in poems. It was simply extant. The temperature of the air around it.

Because if I squint—she felt a plastic smile—because if I squint I can make them look just like perfect apples, neutral and unblemished.

When she was finished smiling she sent Gil an email.

However much she took out, she would need to repay it quickly with money from the cider operation.

She looked at the date. She looked at her finances. It was about time. She could get rid of Jan whenever it suited her.

Within twenty minutes Gil had replied. They would meet at a bar, Tuesday evening, eight o'clock.

Jan figured tagging along to see Gil would be a good chance to get them both off the farm and into the world. Besides, he might be able to take the old man aside to make sure he kept a close eye on Anna after he left. He wasn't sure if he was going to stay for weeks or months—he never thought more than a week ahead—but as she was, it wouldn't be right to leave her alone.

Until then he tried to stay out of her way. He spent more time writing as the autumn work slowed. It was a good day for them both when the plastic jugs arrived. They came in a small white box truck that was still too big to drive up the orchard without cleaving off branches, so Jan and Anna came to the end of the driveway with the utility trailer and helped the driver load box after box onto its bed.

The driver had a half-shaven red beard and seemed tired. He smelled like stale cigarettes and sipped slowly from a Dunkin' Donuts coffee cup. He hardly said a word. Before he left he handed Jan a paper invoice. Jan thought about giving it to Anna, but when he saw Anna's rare and visible happiness in the passenger seat as the production of the cider finally appeared real to her, he folded it up and buried it in his pocket. They drove up to the shed. Anna chose a box and cut into the packing tape with her pocketknife. She held up an empty jug.

"We can finally start pressing," she said.

"That's right."

He watched her turn it around in her hands. He'd chosen jugs with square bases and handles that sloped inward. She marveled at these qualities. With a strange tenderness she rubbed her thumb over the phrase I GAL which was embossed gently near the lid. She smelled inside the jug then lifted it up for Jan to sniff.

He sniffed it, unsure of what else to do, the way you play along with a child. It smelled like plastic.

Nothing got easier. The trees were now almost completely bare. There was little reason to go out into the orchard anymore. Their work revolved around cider production and the unpleasant whine of the squeezebox press.

They cut the black rotting sections off the windfall and loaded what remained onto the racks. Anna insisted on cleaning it thoroughly, so each night they wiped down the racks with bleach water. For his own sanity Jan invited Sean up some days. He didn't help, but hung around the shed talking while they worked. Jan had piqued his interest in art. He'd started attending some of the free lectures at the university. Anna didn't seem to mind his presence. She didn't seem happy about it either.

But it was on a day they were alone when Anna asked Jan:

"What do you really think? Should I print some banners for the farmers market?"

He had to be careful. No sense getting stuck on this.

"What's the point?" he said. "You're almost out of apples."

Anna nodded. She transported full jugs of cider on a dolly to the coolers while Jan thought about his answer.

She came back with the empty dolly.

"I want to keep going to the markets in the winter," she said. "Selling cider."

He took a moment to think while scooping pomace out of a rack and into the compost.

"I guess that makes sense," he said. "Yeah. I'm not the orchardist. Whatever you think is right." He righted the rack again and tried to go on as indifferently as possible. "Why don't you paint a sign?"

He kept working. He looked down. He felt his pulse. After a moment had passed and she still hadn't responded he glanced up. She was staring at him eyes blank and wide.

"I threw out my supplies," she said.

He knew. "You can always buy more."

"Why don't you buy some?" Anna said with sudden venom. "If you want me to paint a sign so badly."

He plunged his rag into the bleach water. No gloves. A little burn. He had to think again. The smell made him a bit dizzy.

"Maybe," he said.

Hard silence as they finished cleaning. When they were done, Jan went inside to shower. He wanted to get the bleach smell off of him before they went to meet Gil at the bar. He folded his clothes on top of the toilet tank, turned on the sink faucet, and ran his wrists under the water. He'd been careless. She still wasn't ready to talk about painting, to remember she was still a person with passion, histories, relationships, opinions. A person who had participated in the world. He got in the shower. In ordinary circumstances he would have already bought her paints, brushes, canvases, whatever she needed, but he had long since run out of money.

It wasn't that he believed she had some kind of special talent, not at all, it was just that painting was the only thing that had ever lifted the spirit of his friend who otherwise spent her days languishing and suffering in her bedroom—or now, languishing and suffering in the dirt. Really she was a failed painter. She had never accessed the material success of her peers or been able to talk about the ideological or technical basis of her close-up paintings of trees. She couldn't even spit out some half-assed art school answer. Whenever she was asked serious questions about her work, her brown eyes that always looked like they were about to cry would just tremble…she'd always been so childish. He felt that Anna craved simplicity while real art required complexity. And what frustrated him about her was how she acted like simplicity was the real thing all along, that her failed art career was besides the point, when really she was just a brat, unable to look failure in the eye. It was only by looking failure in the eye you could overcome it. That was what he believed. "Never cared for ambition"…she was full of shit.

Besides, he thought coldly, I'm going to write a book that grasps the whole world, something full and fearless, sensitive and unafraid, while Anna wants to empty herself of life completely. How could I have thought staying with her would be productive? He was practically her caretaker. It was impossible to focus. He'd hoped it would be like staying with a sweet, amateurish young Burchfield…and why empty herself of life? He remembered the pretty folds of fat on her cheeks when she used to smile, really smile, not whatever voidface she was making these days, her happiness, her sensitivity, her voluptuous way of indulging in the world when she forgot she should be suffering. There was life all around Anna trying to get in and it was like she didn't know what to do with it: like she wanted to hold all the life in her hands and watch it melt away into black water, like she was afraid to let anything vitalize her.

After he had finished washing himself, he wrapped a towel around his waist and climbed the ladder to his room. He checked the time. He wouldn't have time to style his hair. It'd have to just be poofy at the bar. He rifled through his bag to find some clean clothes. He found his flask and drank a little vodka to soothe his headache. He looked sadly at where Victor had slept while screwing the cap back on, missing the easy, uncomplicated company of another man. He glanced out the window.

It seemed Anna had found a small ditch in the dirt near the packing shed. She was curled up in it like an animal, contorting her body in some pose between sitting and lying down, unwilling, it seemed, to wash up or put herself together before they left. He sighed. Then he looked all around the farm. Despite the strange psychological effect it seemed to have had on Anna, the orchard, especially from up here, wasn't nearly as transcendentally remote as she'd described in her email. There were the sheep and the horse farms nearby, sure, but leaving the orchard you only had to make two turns before finding the same familiar strip of shops you saw anywhere else in America: a Starbucks, a Rite-Aid, a Jiffy Lube, a Blue Rat, and a Sunoco were all within two miles of the property. Even at the orchard you could hear cars passing all the time. The world was everywhere, its trucks and cigarettes and smog.

He'd even walked to the Blue Rat one afternoon after they'd fought. As usual, Anna had been trying to get him to act some kind of way he didn't understand, as though his normal way of being was somehow unacceptable to her. He'd just needed to blow off some steam. He remembered how he'd tried to pick up the clerk who sold him rollies, her messy blonde hair and her septum piercing, not really his type but straightforward, friendly, refreshing…it hadn't worked out. They'd just smoked together on the curb after her shift, watching the cars in the hot night while she complained about being stuck in such a shithole town.

Remembering that day made him feel disgusted with himself. I always seek shit out like that even in a place of beauty, he thought, feeling weird, as though the thought came from beyond him. Even if it wasn't so remote, he stilled liked listening the frogs and crickets at night…he believed in his heart that friendship was the only pure way of relating and he was always corrupting it, even with Anna, not that she was particularly beautiful either, except when she was angry, then there was something about her, that life, but how was it she never got lonely? He winced. Christ, he thought, listen to me. The woods can't cleanse me either. All I'm good for is tossing cigarettes and Budweiser cans in the grass.

Suddenly Jan heard a car. He looked out the window. A white sedan was rolling up the gravel driveway.

He saw Anna slowly stand up. She looked down and as if seeing herself for the first time brushed the dirt off her pants.

Jan hurried to finish getting dressed. By the time he joined them outside, Anna had already taken them to the storage shed. There was an older man in a short-sleeve button-down, a woman with oily black hair, and two kids: a young girl who looked about ten in a floral-print dress and cardigan, and a toddler sleeping on the woman's hip.

"Are you sure?" the man said.

The woman glared at him.

"Yes," said Anna. "I'm sorry."

"But it says you're open twelve to four." He was squinting at his phone. "What kind of orchard doesn't let you pick your own apples?"

"This one," said Anna. "I'll have to change it. There used to be a farmstand."

"What's the point?"

"Dad, cut it out," said the woman. "You should be happy she's willing to sell to you at all." She gave Anna a purposeful look. "I'm sorry."

Anna opened one of the coolers where Jan knew what few fancy-grade apples they had left were kept. She picked up a Teratourgima and handed it to the woman.

"These are the ones?" said Anna.

"Yes! Look, Charlotte. See how big they are."

Anna handed it to the little girl.

The kid's eyes, which had looked dead and bored, widened. She took the apple. She could barely hold it. Her hands looked like little mice paws with the apple in them.

Anna took out her phone.

"Two buckets?"

The woman nodded.

"Two buckets is $32.10," she said. "They're an expensive variety."

The woman shook her head. "No, these are the ones. Thank you."

The man said, "Give me a break."

"We have cider, too," Jan said. "Fresh."

"Cider!"

They asked to try some. Anna smiled at Jan as she went to get a glass from the kitchen. He retrieved a jug they had just sealed that morning. It was unlabeled, something that had bothered Jan, but not

Anna, and maybe she was right, because the family didn't seem to care or even notice. He poured out some cider in the glass. It had a nice, deep color. The woman took a long sip, then the man. It was difficult to tell what they thought of it. After a moment, the woman asked for a single jug, and Anna fetched them a fresh one, charged them just under $44, and watched with Jan as the family departed with their goods.

He looked at Anna.

She was incandescent. She was watching the empty driveway with her look of radiance, fulfillment, life.

Involuntarily Jan smiled too. Anna took a celebratory swig of the sample jug, then made a face. "It's not as good as the last batch," she said. "Fizzy, more sour than sweet." Jan laughed and said, Well, that's all right, they bought it anyway. Maybe this one's more of an acquired taste. She nodded. She asked Jan if he wanted to take a sip. He did not. He wanted to keep the vodka on his tongue. They stuck the jug back in the fridge then, since they were late to meet Gil, hurried on their way into town.

17

The truth was it was possible he'd lose Tamara as well as the sheep, Gil was thinking over his beer, after all, neither had kids, they hadn't been married long for their age, only fifteen years, both of them in their late thirties when they'd tied the knot, Tamara on her second marriage and Gil his first. Separation would be easy, compared to others. That was why Tamara's cold distance from the animals had never made sense to him: since they had no children or family he had poured his paternal instinct into the flock. He thought animals deserved paradise, that they were lucky in that they could be spared from our world, yes, amid so much suffering the one thing a person can do is construct a paradise for animals, live happily with the knowledge they've given another being a perfect life, the perfect life everybody deserves, a life of sun and grass, clover and moonlight, free from danger or suffering, born in alfalfa and dead by daisies, cool water from a clean trough, sensible enclosures, gardens, food and space, he loved when the sheep pushed their pink muzzles into his hands, sheep who trusted him to keep them healthy and dry and well-fed, who frolicked even in old age, not too different from him, sheep who forgave instantly, sheep who asked for nothing but protection, sheep as eternal children, their infinite happiness, life-without-sorrow, meadows of heaven. But soon Citrouille would be gone, Blue would be gone, Holly, Josephine, Ewelalia, and thinking of Ewelalia he smiled involuntarily, bringing just after it another pulse of sorrow in his heart which made him slump down a little on the barstool. He remembered naming her with Tamara, how for a moment they'd thought of giving all the sheep new Ewe-pun names. Ewenice. Ewegene. Ewelia. Ewecca. All of them had been ridiculous, but Ewelalia had stuck. He couldn't think of a single sheep he felt he could part with. He loved them all.

Tamara had said it wasn't a big deal to lose a few. Other livestock owners sold all the time, in fact it was ridiculous to be so torn up about it. They were a business, not a sanctuary. They're animals. Maybe she was right. She always said what he should really be care about was humanity, though he had never understood what she meant by that. Maybe he did now. It had resurfaced in their argument: he'd said selling the sheep to some mutton operation was as good as killing them; she'd said let them, they were only animals, you have always refused to look death in the eye; he'd said he'd never understood how she could work at a place like that; she'd said well maybe you ought to try to understand, her deep voice fracturing, the slammed rattle of their flimsy wood door. He'd tried in the past. But he was better with the sheep. Tamara could never get them to listen to her. To trust her. She was too rough with them. They were afraid. When Gil had worked part-time, Tamara had not been able to finish her second inspections of the flock until after nightfall, and both of them had grown lonely, tired, miserable.

No point in reminding her. She knew. He finished his beer. And where was Anna? She was over an hour late and had not responded to his text. Surely young people's sense of time wasn't that different. But there was no sense getting mad about things like that, since secretly he was grateful for the opportunity to get himself together before she came...He didn't like looking vulnerable in front of others, had always felt it was his job to keep spirits together.

He ordered a second beer. They were meeting at the sports bar he'd frequented with Tamara shortly after moving, back when a day's work didn't send them straight to bed. There were lots of neon beer signs: Blue Moon, Modelo, Tecate, Coors Light. The jukebox had a few of Tamara's favorite songs. That made him smile too. He liked all the wood in this bar. Even though the lights were cold, blue and green, the wood gave the place a warm glow.

Whenever the door swung open he smiled with the full force he could muster, looked over, then dropped his happy look with relief when he saw it wasn't Anna. When she did finally arrive, opening the door with her quiet serious way of moving, followed by that man who'd moved in with her, he leapt off his barstool, glued radiance to his face, and went to greet them.

"Anna! It's been too long. Weeks! How are the dogs? How was the harvest? When are we all going a-wassailing?" He turned to the man. Jan. That was his name. "Jan, how are you?"

"Already been drinking, have you?" Jan said and laughed.

Gil laughed too. They all sat down and the kids ordered their own drinks. They talked fast, and from what Gil could gather over the noise of the bar and his thinking, everything seemed to be going well. He couldn't quite hear and was never the type to ask people to repeat themselves. He managed to gather that the harvest hadn't gone perfectly, but that there was reason to be optimistic.

"It's a hard life!" he said, mustering up all his cheer. He patted Anna firmly on her back. "You'll figure things out. Maybe Tamara and I can help you pick next year."

Anna's look changed. She started mumbling about something. He strained to hear. She was saying something about a nature preserve, the old nature preserve. He could hardly hear over all the noise.

"All the pines are new growth," he said. "Those trees are only a few decades old! And of course the fruit trees are even younger."

He hoped that answered whatever she'd asked. Anna nodded flatly and sipped her beer. Jan flagged down the bartender, ordered a pitcher, slapped Gil's back like Gil had slapped Anna's, and laughed heartily. The girl really was the spitting image of Joe, Gil thought: same button nose, same cold dark eyes, top lip fuller than the bottom lip, short and muscular body, strong eyebrows. In Gil's memory Joe was untouched by time. He couldn't remember a single gray hair on that head. Anna's face wasn't long like his had been, her hair quite not as dark. He remembered Joe's death and felt his face deform with grief. His composure was loosened by the beer. To lose both him and Tamara within one year would be too much. He tried to take a drink but the glass was empty.

The worst part of Joe's diagnosis was how he had suddenly seemed so tethered to a world he'd just succeeded in escaping. Abruptly the possibility of living the kind of life he'd always dreamed of was foreclosed. He remembered him saying, one warm night on the porch the summer before his death, how he'd spent so much of his life looking for an exit, a way out, something that would free him from the unpleasant chain of consciousness, and now, as soon as he'd found it, the world decided it would really "happen" to him. He had finally been taken. Gil had tried to comfort his friend but the situation seemed unbearable. It was becoming difficult for Joe to walk. There was no room for anything but despair.

It was only a few weeks later they found him dead in the orchard, his great love, collapsed between two rows of apple trees. His head in the berry bushes. Pinks and reds. Gil had vomited. He'd been exposed three days to the animals and elements.

When he met Anna, Gil instantly understood why Joe had left her the orchard. They were somehow kindred, sharing a certain perspective of the world Joe's daughter always seemed to lack…Gil could never remember the details of that fallout. In Joe's family it almost seemed like familiarity was what bred hatred and unlove: like the less they knew about one another, the more they could somehow bond. Every gradation of knowledge seemed to bring them some kind of pain Gil didn't understand.

Funny I only think things like that when looking at the kid, he thought. She was frowning and listening miserably to something Jan was saying in her ear. It was the same whenever I hung out with Joe, the man made me think about things differently.

Gil frowned too. It was hard not to feel like Anna had killed him a second time in her absolute ignorance of him. And it was hard but ultimately worthwhile to know another person, he really believed that…

He pushed the thought aside. He would just have to have faith she would learn. That's all people can do. He tried to act jolly for them. He slammed his fist down on the bar, patted the kids on the back, offered old memories or bits of "wisdom" whenever it seemed like it would please them. He noticed the pitcher and poured himself more beer. He remembered the flock. Though he'd never admit it, he hated the idea of having the neighbor who had dominated them financially living so close to him. Once construction began, the infinite horizon of the sheep would be closed, their wall of woods knocked down and developed. The little lambs! My baby sheep, spooked by loud machinery. Tamara doesn't even care. She's a killer.

He burst into tears.

His nose filled up with snot. He blew it on the napkin beneath his glass. The kids were looking at him with quiet alarm and so were other people at the bar. The bartender stayed far away, polishing rocks glasses. Gil couldn't get the words out.

By way of explanation he tried to show them a photo of Ewelalia. His glasses were foggy so it was difficult to pull up the photos on his phone. After a moment he got there. Ewelalia! Smiling at the camera with her peach-blossom face, getting her hooves trimmed while leaning back in the blue sling. She was a goofy little sheep. Her sweet silly face. He turned the phone around.

"That's pretty cute!" Jan said. He laughed. "You had me worried."

Anna smiled sadly. She looked down at her hands.

Maybe they hadn't understood. It hurt to be laughed at, but that was fine. He slowly returned his phone to his pocket. Then he felt a weight on his shoulder. He looked up and saw it was Anna's hand. His face was hot. He could feel himself sweating. He caught a glimpse of himself in the mirror behind the bar, and wiped the snot from his nose with a long sleeve.

18

They drove slowly up the hills. They were both drunk and upset. Their headlights lit up the dead plants along the asphalt. It looked a bit like when she first arrived at the orchard. They hardly said a word to each other. When they got inside, Anna stood in the living room. Jan went up the ladder as her eyes adjusted to the darkness.

She went into the kitchen and got a glass of water. Her eyes stung. There was a little bit of moonlight. She took a long, lukewarm sip.

Her head hurt. She rubbed her forehead. Her heart was pounding. She wasn't tired at all. She paced back and forth a bit in the kitchen, hearing the house creak under her footsteps. Upstairs she could faintly hear Jan snoring.

Even though her head was pounding, her body felt calm. Her hate felt cold. She watched slowly and curiously as certain images arrived. The humiliation of being with a person like Jan at the bar. A place she didn't belong anyway. His ugly laughter.

He had acted—so grossly—like a man.

She felt giddy and intoxicated by images that were coming to her, flashing in her mind like light from explosions: erasing Jan's image with the violence of a gunshot: blotting him out like bleach on film: I paint over him, I destroy him: I knock down the firepit and the artificial pond: and everything dormant and unbirthed and abandoned as it had been when she arrived: on the precipice of spring but not really there, stuck in non-time maybe, a non-season: it'll be as if he never came: and silence will reign over everything.

She climbed the ladder to his room. There he was, a mound in the darkness. She shook him awake.

"Jan."

He stirred. Squinting in the night she could see his long lashes fluttering.

"Jan, you have to go."

"What?"

"You have to leave."

Jan hesitated. He reached his hand out into the darkness and it found Anna's thigh. His hands were sweaty. His touch was firm. She moved his hand away.

"No."

The darkness went on. She heard him breathing.

"I can do the rest alone," she said. "You're not needed."

Then Jan turned on his new lamp and sat up against the wall. His face looked small, red, and scared.

"So start packing," she said.

"Packing?"

"I'm going to do it alone."

"Why do you keep saying that?" he said quietly. He climbed out from under his blankets and sat on the edge of the bed. "What do you need? Let me help you."

He'd put it as gently as he could. But it didn't matter how softly he spoke or how much he pretended to care: if Jan hadn't come up, time would have flowed like water.

Jan broke the stillness by rubbing his eyes. He stood up and went to his jacket on the back of his chair and got a cigarette from the pocket. He opened the window and sat by it and lit one. He held the pack out to her but she didn't move.

He was buying time. He took two long drags and then spoke.

"Anna, I'm practically out of money. I spent half of it getting up here and the other half buying us things."

"I'll give you money."

"I'd rather have a few weeks to get the manuscript in order."

"You have to go."

"Anna, I have nowhere to go."

"That's not true."

He fiddled with the cigarette filter in his hand. "I mean nowhere like this."

He glanced up at her, suddenly heated.

"Spare me one of your episodes. I'm the one person who missed you enough to insist on visiting, and you're seriously going to kick me out in the middle of the night?"

She didn't reply. Suddenly she felt tired and confused. Breeze and a sweet smell from the night window mixed with smoke. Jan held her gaze for a while then looked away again.

"I know this hasn't been sustainable for our friendship," he said, "and I'm sorry if I haven't seemed appreciative of what you've done for me. I do appreciate it."

He fiddled with the cigarette in his hands.

"Sean's made some friends who want to talk to me about the project. I can call and see if I can stay with them for a few days—or with him. And you can think about it." He paused. "I don't want to leave for good."

"I don't care where you go."

Jan looked at her for a long time. She was not thinking about anything. Her anger was blank. She suffered under the weight of his emotions and eventually she had to look down.

She heard Jan shut the window. "I'll call Sean in the morning," he said.

When she woke up he was already gone.

She felt good and fresh. She didn't regret it. It felt cool inside the cabin, easy to breathe.

She went upstairs just to make sure. His bed was made. His backpack and his computer were gone, but his luggage was still there. Victor's bed was still made too.

She really didn't regret it. And if she did she obliterated the thought. That'll be a skill to resharpen, she told herself. Obliteration. Because when she did it it was a bit difficult. A bit painful. No, nothing. Interesting how something can end so plain and so clean. Good.

She took the sheets off Jan's bed and stacked his mattress on top of the others. She brought the sheets downstairs to be washed, but first she had to take the wet clothes out of the washing machine to dry them on the clothesline. They smelled lovely, like flowers.

She looked at the time: 8:24.

Eight in the morning and I'm alive again, she thought.

She went to make herself breakfast. As she went to the fridge, she saw that Jan had scribbled something on a sheet of paper and stuck it beneath a magnet.

It was his label idea. It took her a few seconds to make out the image. He had drawn a woman collapsed in the earth with spirals for eyes and drawn her extra curvy, much curvier than she was, with her breasts smooshed up against the grass. Four sticks Anna supposed were paintbrushes emerged from between her knuckles. They made it look like the woman had claws. The proportions were all wrong. He was a terrible artist.

According to the pamphlets the loan office had emailed her, a visually striking label on a farm product could increase sales by up to thirty percent.

She wanted to throw it away, but it was worth thinking about. The idea of degrading herself for money wasn't completely unattractive, so long as it was all outside her.

She remembered she hadn't gotten a chance last night to ask Gil about the loan mentorship. She remembered his snotface and pitied him: hard to imagine someone like that in a position to help.

She set the paper down on the table.

It didn't bother her. She was feeling optimistic about her ability to make money without Jan. Lighthearted for the first time in weeks. She willed it. Morning colors falling on the wood. Sunshine.

In the refrigerator there wasn't much food left. She fixed herself some coffee, some cider, some yogurt and walnuts. She had gotten used to the strange taste of the dark and sour cider, but could only eat a few bites of food. Her stomach felt weak.

After pressing two hours' worth of jugs, she thought, maybe I'll take the rest of the day off. That seemed like a good idea. She would lie in the grass between two rows of trees and renew herself. That's right. Marry the money-self and the soothed-self, somehow. Alone, the balancing act would be possible. It was the presence of others that had made life so difficult, same as it been all her life. Why had that taken so long to understand? She was still the same person.

She went outside. She fetched one of the watering cans by the porch and filled it up with water from the blue rain barrel. She watered the plants in the garden. The beans, horseradish, and toad lilies were blooming and ripening. Their colors were beautiful and bright. With the same can, she replenished the dogs' water bowl. Then she started walking towards the ducks to give them their water and let them out for the day.

But on her way to the coop she saw the door was already open. In the dirt beside the chicken wire three duck hens lay dead. They had been eviscerated and half-eaten by some animal. Their necks were all mangled, and in the hole of one's breast she could see the faint rainbow of its organs, yellow purple and red. The hens in their dresses.

She felt nauseous. Her stomach pinched and turned.

One nervous hen was trembling in the run. The others must have scattered.

She looked all around. The orchard radiated out from her like a ripple in water. Maybe.

Yes, here and there she could see some more ducks. One was preening on a rock.

But the bear never came around anymore. It was gone.

She tried to stay calm.

If the orchard were a cathedral, the twelfth bell would have been pealing.

Crows cawed in trees. She remembered: their black caws. The pretty morning light.

A duck is a thing you eat, she thought. Dead animals are no tragedy.

Not red, brown, like terracotta.

And then the orchard answered her. She located them as a camera locates its subject. The two dogs were chasing each other in the far grass, bounding and cantering like young horses. She saw Pell first, then Midge with her bloodstained maw.

She whistled for them and they came.

The dogs' eyes looked black and tiny. There was no love in them. Anna's vision was blurry. No, there was love. The dogs were looking up at her with love and blankness. She crouched down in Midge's face with a swift, violent movement. She smacked the dog on its nose. Pell ducked his tail between his legs and slipped away.

Midge's tail went between her legs, too, but she kept trying to wag it against the soft skin of her stomach, and she licked her bloody lips as she looked back up at Anna. Anna tried to pick her up by her scruff and legs, but she tripped over the dog. She was too heavy. The dog yelped as the two of them stumbled in the grass. She smacked the dog on the ear. It yelped again. Anna tried again. She managed to lift her. She felt it squirming. She was taking it to its cage. She never put the dogs in their cages, after all, they were free, but she was taking it to its cage, blood and all, until she could figure out what to do with it, whether it would need to die, she was taking it to its cage, she was going to throw her in her cage, she walked past the cage, they went into the bedroom, they collapsed on the unmade bed together and Anna stroked the frightened bloody animal until the afternoon.

She sat down on the cabin steps with her phone in her hand. She felt overheated. She took her jacket off. She wondered what Tamara would say. She imagined Tamara inspecting Midge's muzzle with the cold precision of a surgeon, like she had in the woods, then looking at Anna with disgust. Reducing her to the image of a failure. Maybe she'd kill the dog. Maybe Midge had a taste for duck blood and couldn't be kept alive. Country people are like that, aren't they? It was the time of death.

    She dialed.
    Two, three, four rings.
    No response.
    She rang again.
    "Hello?"
    "Hi, Tamara."
    "What do you need? Gil's still asleep."
    She winced.
    "Anna?"
    "I don't need anything. Never mind. See you soon."

Tamara stood in front of her kitchen sink. She thought about calling back. Probably better to ask Gil how the night had gone first.
    She was looking out the window at a field, where a dog was standing off with a black bear who had ambled quietly up to the fence. The dog gave three big barks. The bear ran away startled.
    She brought Gil his glass of water. He was snoring on the couch. Pisco, one of the border collies, was curled up around his legs. Tamara tried to smile at Pisco. She held out her hand. The dog

sniffed around for something to eat and, finding nothing, growled a little, then tucked its face into Gil's side.

Tamara stood watching them for a long time. Whatever feeling came she pushed back down with a firm hand. When she felt she had sufficiently quelled them, she returned to work.

19

Anna stayed sitting on the steps for a while, holding her phone in her hand. She was trying not to think about anything. Nothing. It was very quiet. She brushed dirt off the wood and set her phone down. The bamboo and dead grass were swaying in the wind.

She should dispose of the duck corpses before flies came to lay maggots.

But she probably only had a day until Jan came back for the rest of his things, and she was suffused with a desire to capitalize on that solitude.

She felt nauseous still. Nauseous and sentimental.

She picked up her phone and stood up. She walked to the greenhouse. The plants had been forgotten and were wilting. She opened the cabinet, brushing away dust and cobwebs. So the desire had been building. He didn't have to be wrong about everything. Just don't think. She surveyed her supplies. Five or six hog-bristle brushes, some old oil paints, linseed oil, a bottle of turpentine, an easel, a palette and knife, canvases. She took a 16x16, dumped some gear into a plastic bucket, and tucked the easel and canvas beneath her arm.

The phthalo green was almost empty, shriveled up like the plants. She liked expensive paints: Sennelier when she could afford it, as though nicer paints might make up for what she knew she lacked in talent.

Even with just a little green for those iridescent feathers, she figured she could probably make it work. Besides, there were a million ways to mix it. Green was a luxury.

She left the greenhouse with her gear and started setting up her easel in front of the corpses. She could maybe regain something in their death. Their dead wonder.

But the nausea wouldn't go away. Looking at the gore again she almost vomited.

Then why not paint the orchard? She was used to painting trees. Maybe even good at it. The trees she was used to painting were imaginary. She rarely used references, didn't even like to do studies. So then, she thought smiling: make room for the new. And since it was autumn, she wouldn't need to use much green at all: just enough to breathe some life into the gray of branches.

She gathered her things again and crested the hill to the orchard. Now deep in autumn the color of the small hills looked mute and desolate, brown and gray and black, though some brilliant red leaves still burned here and there. Her back ached. The easel was heavy and cumbersome. She set it up again in a row of Federations. The wood of the easel looked so much warmer than the wood of the trees.

She would try to paint thoughtlessly.

She would try humbly to be like Burchfield. The name stung as it crossed her mind. Not ambitiously, she thought alarmed, no need for ambition: just to see something else in a treescape: spring-within-autumn as he had seen September-within-August: the gateway to the more beautiful world: wetness, rainbows, springtime, peace: the possibility of a flight-forward: the new escape.

She looked at the painting supplies and tried to think about them, and to access something in her own thinking about them.

Here are the items that constituted my existence. No organic stretch of being, no extension of my body into its sparkling components. These are things you can buy at the store. Things you can have delivered. Could that be comforting? Maybe. Let's start with the sky. It's blue today, the most strident color of the day. It's a day when blue imposes its own unity, no clouds, because on clear days like today I can make a square with my two hands, as if framing a shot for a photograph, extend those hands upward toward the heavens, and capture it purely in my hands: blue.

Her hand shook as she dragged the palette knife around, mixing blue and white. Then she filled up the canvas with hesitant little strokes.

Now the branches. Her paintings had been of trees so close up you couldn't at first tell that they were trees. She liked for them to seem abstract until you looked closely and saw they weren't. Looking at the branches of the apple trees and trying to make a painting out of them was harder. Easy to make the abstract tangible, difficult to make the tangible abstract. She found she knew too much about the buds and shoots for them to transmute into movement and feeling: for instance, looking at those clean snips where they had pruned, how the fireblight had spread from tree to tree. She knew: they hadn't sterilized the pruners. The orchard was a thing she'd harmed. What she was doing wasn't too different from painting dead ducks.

As if to apologize, though she was tempted to go for those bold, glowing colors she'd always liked, she tried to remain faithful to the true colors of the world.

It would really be nice to have some green. Pigments are recombinant, made from the stuff of life: pigments come from the world. Dig up soil, find red rocks, grind them down. Woad for indigo. Green was harder. There was no easy way to make a green that would last. But why does it need to last? Don't get ambitious. The color of life! She stood thinking about all this, still afraid to paint the first branch. Still feeling sick.

Just start with a branch.

She mixed the sad gray color that was the branch.

Block out the light and shadow. Where to start? There was a video she used to watch whenever she felt nervous, something from her earliest days of study. With an anxious sigh she took her phone out of her pocket and tried to watch it. It wouldn't load. No signal.

Annoyed, she tossed the phone in the grass.

Trust yourself, that's right. Muscle memory. She scooped up some of the gray paint with a filbert brush and made some hesitant strokes on the canvas. But then she saw that she had applied too much, and a huge glob of paint was dripping downwards, like the dead orchard was itself leaking blood. The pool of paint dripped down and landed in the grass.

She felt disoriented…

She realized she was in a lot of pain. She closed her eyes. Because this was my way of trying to be in the world, because I never felt right in the world except when painting over my field of vision…blue, blue, blue. I wanted to see and not be seen. It was the one thing that made me feel like I wasn't dying.

But I do still feel like dying, she thought slowly. Right now. I want to be nobody and a painter is somebody.

She opened her eyes and looked at the painting.

I want to see things in a way that's impossible…I want the most primordial, essential vision…it feels impossible to forget, even in a place like this, because that little gray stroke doesn't look like nothing anymore. It was supposed to be an anonymous branch and it looks like the dead gray arm of a person, a lover or an enemy. Or the barrel of the gun in my attic.

After all, a painting is a thing of the world. What am I supposed to do once it's in the world?

She knelt and wet her fingers with saliva. She tried to rub the paint that had dripped off the grass, but it wouldn't come off. So she ripped up the grass instead, gagging.

She stood up again. She looked at the painting. Nothing. Violence flooded her. She beat the painting off the easel. It landed in the dirt near her phone.

No, of course not.

20

She was loading apples into the press and trying not to vomit when her phone went off. It was eleven o'clock the morning after she had tried to paint. Her phone had gone off once already, but she hadn't heard it over the loudness of the machine. She picked up. It was Jan.

"Hello?" she said.

There was some noise from his side. She walked out of the shed and into the sunshine.

"Hi Anna," he said finally. He sounded like he had been laughing. A few more seconds passed, and then he sounded serious. "How are you?"

"I'm fine."

"Good," said Jan. He hesitated.

Anna's stomach felt weak. She slunk down against the wall of the shed.

"I have something to ask," said Jan.

"Then ask it." She was dizzy.

"The people I'm staying with want to come up and see the orchard," he said. He paused again. "Um," he said. There was no background noise anymore. He was quiet on the line.

He couldn't be serious. She didn't answer.

"Sean told them all about it. Now they won't let the idea of seeing it go."

"Jan, that's not my problem."

"I'll try to convince them to buy something," he said.

He sounded like he didn't mean it, but that did make her pause. It was silent between them.

"They'll buy things, I'll get my stuff, we'll be out," he said.

She was listening to the last birds.

"Anna?"

"All right."

"Thank you. It's just that I don't want them to think I'm difficult, that there's some reason I wouldn't be allowed up. You know what I mean?"

She pressed her two fingers against her forehead.

"That's fine," she said. "I don't care."

Her stomach was twisting.

"Thank you, Anna," Jan said quietly.

If Jan wanted to bring guests to the orchard, maybe they wouldn't have to confront each other again. He could get his things while everybody pantomimed friendship. Life would resume easily. No hard goodbyes.

"But they better not leave shit in the fields," she added.

No response from Jan.

"You know what I mean?"

"You got it."

He hung up.

Her nausea flared. She vomited in the grass. After rinsing out her mouth in the bathroom, she went back to the cider press. She wanted a dozen more jugs before Saturday's market.

They came in the late afternoon. There were two cars, Jan's and a blue Subaru. Jan and Sean got out of the first car. Two men and a woman got out of the second. The woman was wearing a long gray skirt and a linen button-down. She had short auburn hair. The men and Sean wore jeans, sneakers, and sweaters. All five had backpacks with them. They were all young and smiling.

"Anna, this is Scott, Valerie, and Omar," Jan called from across the grass. "And you already know Sean."

She greeted them. She and Jan shared a limp hug. When they were done hugging she glanced at his face. His eyes were painted with the friendly look you reserve for your acquaintances. They communicated nothing.

At the kitchen table everybody praised the beauty of the farm. They were all so excited to see it in such pretty gold light. They opened beers, talked loudly, laughed, and asked Anna the usual questions about growth, harvest, happiness, money, and solitude. She noticed Sean's excitement to be hanging out with older students. She had never noticed before how he gazed at Jan with quiet admiration whenever he spoke, as if Jan were illuminating the world for him. *I don't understand the world and it frightens me* was all she had ever heard from Sean. When did that change? The fearful look from his eyes had vanished. Everyone was listening to Jan discuss some detail about his manuscript. It seemed he had already filled them in on the gist of it. He was speaking quickly, happy in the limelight. She knew him well enough to tell he felt ambiguously about them, that he felt both anxious for their approval and vaguely superior to them, like he knew he had things they wanted. Eventually he probed them for some information about twentieth-century America pertaining to a moment in Burchfield's life. Scott provided it, speaking with a deep, slow, intelligent voice.

Jan seemed to be drinking up every word.

Whenever she caught his eye, he just looked at her neutrally.

What was he thinking? She felt miserable, shut out.

Her stomach cramped up again.

They kept talking. She found it hard to keep up. History had always slipped by her. Who even were these people? Why is it that things just happen, she thought, that people walk into my life based on sheer proximity, even out here in the middle of nowhere? I have no say in anything that happens, it's awful. Even if chance has been kind to me, I hate it.

Not that there wasn't part of her even now that could try to access some of that happiness. She didn't like feeling left out in her own home, not at all. She tried to dredge up a little humanity. She drank a little beer, made a little joke. Someone laughed. She smiled. A sprout of connection: that feeling people are supposed to feel. She thought: from time to time I can feel what people are supposed to feel.

Probably Jan would encourage her. She looked at him for his approval.

But Jan was staring at the others with the hungry look he used to reserve for her. Scott, then Omar, then finally Valerie. A long look for Valerie.

He was inaccessible.

Anna caught Jan's eye again. She tried to look at him sadly, communicate some degree of suffering.

Jan's face stayed blank.

Then he winked at her.

And the night went on. Though she tried twice to bring it up, nobody was particularly interested in seeing what she had for sale. When she tucked some hair behind her ear, she felt the sick sweat on her forehead.

"Are you all right?" Omar asked.

Everyone turned to look at her.

"Yes," she said. Her voice was hoarse. "I'm going to sleep. Excuse me."

"Farmers sleep early!" Valerie said.

"It's all just too much for Anna," Jan said.

Everyone laughed.

She brought a bucket with her to bed to vomit in. The night continued without her. The pain kept her awake. She listened to their long conversations. She heard people fracturing and connecting, fracturing and connecting.

She had to pee but she was afraid to walk through the living room to the bathroom. She didn't want to be seen looking as sick as she did. She tossed and turned in her sheets. She was sweating.

When she woke up she was in bad stomach pain. She got out of bed and rushed to the bathroom, where dead leaves had blown in from the open window. On her way, she saw Valerie passed out on the couch. The rest of them must be asleep upstairs. The air had the stale scent of hangovers.

She collapsed on the toilet. It was diarrhea. Looking at it, she saw that there was blood.

She stood still in the bathroom, where she felt safe and locked away from the others. But there was nothing to do but drive to the doctor.

Anna slipped into the kitchen to try to sip water before leaving. Empty beer bottles and wine glasses littered the wood table. She stepped in something sticky. As she poured herself a glass she heard Valerie stir. She froze. When she was sure she wasn't waking up, Anna snuck out the door, got in her car, and drove.

There was a Minute Clinic at the CVS, which was closer, but she did not want to go to a CVS, so she decided to drive to a clinic thirty-five minutes away. There was a lot of traffic on the clinic's street. It was a big, busy street. Telephone lines lined the sidewalk. There were many wide lanes in the road. At a red light, she watched someone with a plastic bag try to cross the enormous crosswalk. Its walk signal was counting down from seventy-three. The billboards advertised fast food, Walmart, motels, gas prices. It was a very annotated part of town, she thought. Annotated. The land seemed very flat. It was hard to believe there were hills and farms and streams and forests just a few miles away. The light changed and she almost drove on, but first she had to wait for another line of cars to take their left turns. It was hot for October. The sun baked the asphalt and hurt her eyes. Finally it was her time to go. She pulled into the clinic, which was at the edge of a strip of stores before a highway overpass.

The clinic was pleasantly dim-lit. There was a fake houseplant in the corner of the room and a low coffee table with magazines. She went to the counter where a woman sat behind a computer.

"What are you here for today?"

"Vomiting and diarrhea."

"You poor thing," the woman said sweetly. "Are you a new patient?"

"Yes."

She answered a few more questions. Allergies, none. Insurance, no. Emergency contact. She hesitated. She put down Tamara's number. Would it be okay—to do that? But who else?

The woman typed up her replies and sometimes she had to repeat herself. Another woman sneezed in the waiting area.

The woman nodded while Anna tried to discern her expression.

"All right. We have a form to fill out," she said, handing Anna the clipboard.

After completing the form she thought about how to entertain herself. She looked through the magazines on the coffee table. *People, Elle, Better Homes & Gardens, TIME,* and *InStyle.* Do people even read these anymore? she thought. She flipped through *Better Homes & Gardens* but couldn't focus on any of the articles. Instead she looked at her phone until the doctor called. He gave her fluids. He joked about how it used to be, how she was lucky she wasn't leaving with a plastic cup with a screw-on lid.

She paid for her visit and then left. She stood on the sidewalk with her receipt.

She checked her phone again. No messages.

She got back in her car. I guess I should try to eat something, she thought. She had barely eaten at all in the past few days. And maybe a cup of coffee would stimulate her bowels, help her stomach pass whatever was festering in there.

She drove down the road looking for a place to eat. Dry grass struggled to survive in the medians. Finally she was at a stretch of restaurants. She could take her pick: Arby's, Burger King, Subway, Cracker Barrel, Wendy's, Popeyes, McDonald's.

There were a few cars in line at the McDonald's drive-thru: two sedans, an SUV, and a truck. She pulled into line behind them. She idled in her car. She really hoped she would be able to stomach whatever they had for her. She still felt queasy. She pulled up the menu on her phone. A Southwest Salad would probably get her some fiber, but for some reason, Anna was really craving a cheeseburger.

She watched a woman leave McDonald's balancing two bags of food in one arm. Her other arm dragged along a boy in a Hot Wheels T-shirt.

Now it was Anna's turn to order. The worker apologized for the wait.

"Not a problem," said Anna. "I'll take a McDouble, a large fries, and a coffee."

"Cream and sugar?"

"Sure."

When she pulled up to the second window to get her food, she looked into the restaurant. There was a teenager shaking potatoes around in the deep fryer. Then the window opened. She smiled at the cashier. She accepted her food. It smelled great.

ACKNOWLEDGEMENTS

Thank you to Jamison Murphy and Benjamin Crais, who helped me through this manuscript from its earliest draft.

Thank you to all the mentors, friends, and loved ones who read and offered feedback, encouragement, and advice on this book, including Rebecca Gearhart, Naïma Msechu, Phillip Spinella, PJ Lombardo, Alex Reubert, Jessica Bouvier, Sara Judy, Francisco Robles, Katherine Hur, Steve Tomasula, Ryan Ruby, Jim Grimsley, Deborah Elise White, José Quiroga, Roy Scranton, Azareen Van der Vliet Oloomi, Joyelle McSweeney, Johannes Göransson, Lauren Cerand, Sam Higgins, Patrick Cottrell, Janice Lee, Farbod Kokabi, Zoe Darsee, Suzanne Doogan, Shane McCord, and Stone Filipczak.

Thank you to Meg Reid and everyone else at Hub City.

Thank you to Joseph Grantham, Ashleigh Bryant Phillips, Blake Butler, Megan Boyle, Don Berger, Teddy Rowe, Devin Campbell, and Owen Edwards for being my literary family.

Thank you to Josh Dibb, Lisa Duva, Pete Swanson, Zach Phillips, Annie Loucka, Em Downing, Jan Fontana, Hayes Hoey, Dagmar Zuniga, and Steven Thompson for your wisdom, love, and care when I needed it most.

PUBLISHING
New & Extraordinary
VOICES FROM THE
AMERICAN SOUTH

Celebrating its 30th year in 2025, Hub City Press has emerged as the South's premier independent literary press. Founded in Spartanburg, South Carolina in 1995, Hub City is interested in books with a strong sense of place and is committed to finding and spotlighting extraordinary new and unsung writers from the American South. Our curated list champions diverse authors and books that don't fit into the commercial or academic publishing landscape.

Funded by the National Endowment for the Arts, Hub City Press books have been widely praised and featured in the *New York Times*, the *Los Angeles Times*, NPR, the *San Francisco Chronicle*, the *Wall Street Journal*, *Entertainment Weekly*, the *Los Angeles Review of Books*, the *Boston Globe*, and many other outlets.

Hub City Press books are made possible through the generous support of grants and donations from corporations, state and federal grant programs, family foundations, and the many individuals who support our mission of building a more inclusive literary arts culture, in particular: Byron Morris, Charles and Katherine Frazier, and Michel and Eliot Stone. Hub City Press gratefully acknowledges support from the National Endowment for the Arts, the Amazon Literary Partnership, the South Carolina Arts Commission, Spartanburg County Public Library, and the City of Spartanburg.